I0730451

# CRIMSON

RUTHLESS CLAWS BOOK 2

MAGGIE ALABASTER

Copyright © 2022 by Maggie Alabaster

All rights reserved.

No part of this book may be reproduced in any form or by any electronic or mechanical means, including information storage and retrieval systems, without written permission from the author, except for the use of brief quotations in a book review.

Cover by JoY Design Studio

Edited by Lily Luchesi

Proofread by Nora Hogan

TRIGGER WARNING

NOTE: This book contains one non-con scene and forced sterilisation.

JAKE

*"Fuck."*

Cooper and I stopped around the corner and left my SUV by the side of the road, engine thrumming.

I wanted, needed, to run. My heart thundered. Fear and adrenaline coursed through my body. Too much.

Reluctantly, I put up a trembling hand to keep Cooper at a slow, careful walk. This was exactly when running in blindly could get us killed.

If there was a chance Ivory was still alive…

No. She *had* to be alive. I wouldn't accept anything else. She was infuriating as hells at times, but the woman was my whole fucking world. If she was dead, I might as well be too.

I sniffed the air. The scent of her lingered, white

wolf and lavender perfume. It was faint. She was long gone. Along with a whole fucking pack of black wolves.

Her white Cobra was parked by the side of the road, the door open.

"What—" Cooper started.

"Shhh." I sniffed around again. There was no one here. A human or two somewhere nearby, but not Ivory or her bodyguard, Ben, and not Alastair Dagen.

A smear of mostly dried blood was on the road a few metres from her car. Hers. Another smear lay a few metres away. Ben's.

It wasn't enough to indicate that either of them were dead. They were alive when they were taken from here.

I couldn't smell petrol or any sort of accelerant. I also couldn't rule out a bomb rigged to blow if I touched her car. I stepped close enough to peer inside. Her phone and watch lay on the floor, faintly illuminated by the nearby streetlight.

"Her mother's watch," I said softly. I teased her for not wearing a smartwatch, but she preferred the older technology. And the connection with her mother. "She would want us to get it, but not at the risk of our own lives."

"I'll get it," Cooper said.

I raised my eyebrows at him. When he didn't even flinch, I stood back, hands raised.

"Go for it, Pup." I shouldn't let him take the chance. Ivory would be pissed when she found out. She'd be equally pissed if there was no bomb and I let her watch get stolen.

He moved closer to the car. "How did you know where to find it anyway?"

"I put a tracker on all of her cars," I said unapologetically. "For just this kind of situation."

"Does she know?" He reached in tentatively.

"I don't know," I said. "Probably. It was always hard to fool her."

Cooper nodded. He snatched up the watch, and her phone for good measure, then leapt back.

The car didn't explode.

"How do we find her?" he asked. I didn't need to look at his face to know he was as scared as I was. His voice was laced with it and he smelled of worry and fear. A great combination in an enemy, but not so much in a friend. And one of the guys I shared Ivory with. I knew, at some point, Ben would join us in that too. I thanked the gods he was with her. If anyone could protect her until I rescued her, it was him.

"We do what she asked us to do," I said finally.

"But—" He frowned at me.

"We know who took her," I snapped. "The only chance we have of figuring out where, is to do what she asked." I thought for a moment. "How do you feel about driving a Cobra? She won't want it left here."

"Depends. You think it would explode if I turn the engine on?" He looked at it doubtfully.

"Only one way to find out." I grinned and waved my hand toward the driver's seat.

Cooper frowned but climbed in and closed the door behind him. He turned the key over. The engine purred to life.

I nodded, satisfied. "Follow me back to Crimson. Then we need to get to work."

1

IVORY

I DON'T KNOW which hurt more, my leg or my face. It might be a tie.

I dropped my head and watched blood drip out of the teeth marks on my calf and pool on the floor of the car. Whatever, it wasn't my fucking car. Sure, it was my blood, but chances were, I wouldn't need it much longer.

I glanced over to Ben. He had a similar injury to one of his legs, and claw marks on his chest and back. He was clearly in as much pain as I was. Like me, he was a stubborn prick and was trying not to show it. Neither of us wanted to give Dagen the satisfaction of hearing us scream.

"Where do you think we're going?" he asked, his voice low.

I shook my head and winced at the searing agony that small movement caused.

"I don't know," I managed to say. I didn't know why we were still alive, much less where the asshole was taking us.

Dagen's words, 'You'll learn, bitch,' suggested he intended to keep me alive for a while longer. How much longer was anyone's guess. Given I had no desire to learn anything from Alistair Dagen, he'd probably kill me out of frustration.

My best hope right now was that Jake was doing what I asked him to do. He knew the organisation as well as I did. Better. He'd keep it running. Nothing was stopping Ivory Claw from wiping out the Onyx Ridge Pack now they had moved against me directly, personally. Jake and Cooper would have a field day doing just that. Jake waited nearly two decades for this. My only regret was that I'd miss all the fun.

Ben would, too, come to that. He enjoyed a good killing as much as the next wolf.

"I'm sorry," he said softly. "I should have—"

I would have frowned at him, but my face hurt too badly from where Asshole hit me. Twice. For that alone, I should rip his head off. I would, if I got the chance.

"For what?"

"Letting them touch you." He grimaced toward Dagen, who sat in the front passenger seat.

I waved a couple of fingers in dismissal. "There were sixteen of them and only two of us. If anything, it's my fault for not traveling with an ostentatious-as-shit entourage." I said that last bit loud enough for Asshole to hear me.

He didn't respond.

I lowered my voice again. "The only thing you could have done was kill me. If you did that, you'd have to make sure they killed you right after. Otherwise Jake would hunt down your ass and make your final days a living misery."

Ben managed a pained half-smile. "Yeah, he would, but I would never kill you. Unless you ordered me to. And..." he gestured toward the collar around his neck. Identical to mine, it was to stop us from shifting into wolf form, "this makes it harder."

That was the point, of course. I was sitting in the back of a black SUV, completely naked, but the inability to shift made me feel barer than the lack of clothes. My inner wolf was my better half. Stronger, faster, deadlier.

Without her, I was nothing more than Ivory, head of the biggest criminal organisation in New

South Wales. Okay, that was a lot, but I still needed my wolf to be whole.

"For the record, I wouldn't order you to kill me," I told him. No matter how bad things got, I always managed to find a way out. I would do it this time too.

"That's good." His gaze flicked toward Dagen. He looked like he had something else to say, but shook his head slightly. He looked back at me with meaning in his eyes.

Maybe I should have been taken by surprise, but I wasn't. He was one of my most trusted bodyguards. We'd worked closely together for years. That spilled over into the bedroom a time or two. I may never trust anyone the way I trusted Jake, but Ben was in my top three. Cooper rounded that out, although we'd only known each other a short time. In my line of work, trust was everything.

I reached over and laced my fingers through his. Hopefully Dagen would only assume we were two prisoners consoling each other. A sniff of anything more and he'd use that to his advantage.

"There's a private airfield up this way," Ben said a few minutes later.

I peered through the window. He was right. A road sign read 'private property' but a hangar and a short airstrip appeared as we drove out from behind a series of industrial buildings.

A jet stood outside the hangar. Several cars and people occupied a small carpark.

"Fuck," I said under my breath. I assumed Asshole would take us somewhere in Sydney. That was a big enough haystack to find two needles in. Out of Sydney could mean anywhere in Australia, or even another country.

Hells, he might be planning to make us skydive once we were over the harbour—without a parachute.

Ben's hand tightened on mine.

I turned back toward him questioningly. "Don't like flying?"

He curled his lip, but didn't take his eyes off the window. "Don't like witches."

I didn't know which one of the people standing waiting was a witch, but if he said one of them was, I believed him. His hatred of them was well known. He was orphaned young and raised by witches who had little love for shifters. I didn't blame him for his bitterness. After Dagen's father murdered my parents, I was raised by his aunt. Helen Dagen was as nasty a piece of work as her brother. Having her killed was a pleasure.

"Trust Alistair to be working with witches," I said. I already knew that about him. He was the one who left the set of magic-filled stones at Silas Wheeler's garage.

Ben turned toward me and frowned. "I guess we know what the meaning of the dampening stone was."

Dampening stones stopped a witch from using magic. In this case, it was a message to say he'd found a way to stop us from shifting.

I remembered the last stone and shuddered. Bonding stone. If that was infused with magic, then touched me and one of Dagen's men, or Dagen himself, spilled their cum inside me, it would form an empathic bond between us. The idea of that kind of link with him was even more sickening than the idea of him touching me in the first place.

Judging by the fierce expression on Ben's face, he was thinking the same thing. And was determined not to let it happen.

I appreciated the sentiment and knew he'd die for me, but I preferred not to think too much about it. I would deal with it if and when the time came.

The SUV pulled up near the plane. People swarmed around it, mostly men in black suits. A woman in blue jeans and a cat t-shirt strode along behind them like she owned the airfield. The witch, I assumed.

Ben looked like he desperately wanted to shift and tear her head off, literally.

"Someone you know?" I asked softly. I unwound my hand from his before anyone saw.

"Yeah. Irina." He didn't elaborate. I didn't ask him to. There would be time for that later.

"Get them," Dagen ordered. He opened his own door and moved away from the SUV.

"Gods forbid he got his hands dirty," I said sarcastically.

"Can you stand?" Ben's brow corrugated with concern.

"Not without help," I admitted. "I think I'm about to get some."

One of Asshole's men opened the door and leaned in to grab me. I let him pull me up and out. I almost fell, but another goon moved to the other side of me and slipped an arm under mine.

I looked at him sharply, wanting to tell him to fuck off, but I would have face planted on the ground without help. Being naked in front of about thirty men who loathed me because of what I had done, or who I was, or both, was bad enough. As a shifter, being naked didn't bother me as much as it might bother others, but vulnerability—that bothered me a lot.

Alistair Dagen looked down his long nose at me. I thought he was going to make some triumphant announcement, or gesture that would make all his goons clap, or something inane like that.

Instead, he waved at the witch. "Heal them. I don't want blood in my plane. But leave the bruises on the bitch's face." Of course he was the kind of prick who liked to leave marks.

I rolled my eyes at him, even though it hurt like fuck.

The witch, her expression haughty and unimpressed, stepped toward me. Mercifully, she crouched and started to knit the bone in my leg back together.

Unfortunately that too hurt like fuck and I couldn't keep from crying out in agony.

Dagen smiled.

If not for the goon's tight grip on my arms, I might have lunged at him the moment my leg was fixed.

Instead, I stood and endured in silence while Irina healed my broken cheekbone. Her expression gave away nothing of her thoughts. Not even slightly. If I was carved of ice, she was made of rock.

No, brick. Brick walls could be torn down and left in ruins. She deserved that for working with Asshole.

By the time she stepped toward Ben, all my pain was gone. Another henchman handed me clothes to put on. Track pants and a t-shirt, both too big, but still, clothes.

Ben glared at Irina in disgust when she stepped toward him. He looked like he'd prefer to be in pain than have her touch him.

Now I could frown again, I did just that, sternly.

He gritted his teeth and stood his ground while she healed him of his scratches and scrapes.

The expression of absolute disdain on her face while she did it suggested she remembered him too. For some reason, that bothered me.

Jealousy is an irrational emotion, so I decided on protectiveness instead. Under the circumstances, it made a lot of sense anyway. We were all each other had right now. Us, and what dignity we had left.

I dressed quickly. If I wore pyjamas, they might look like this. Loose and comfortable. I felt around inside a pocket and found a hair tie. They were someone else's clothes then. Irina's perhaps? Whatever, clothes were clothes.

I pulled my hair up and fastened it back out of the way. In the window of the SUV, I caught a glimpse of my reflection. I looked less like big, bad Ivory and more like Elodie, the woman I spent the last nine years putting behind me. My birth name; Jake was the only one who called me that. With the exception of Alistair Dagen, when he was trying to be an even bigger asshole than usual.

I could have been this woman I saw in the glass, had life not turned out differently. Suburban wife and mother— Oh fuck, who was I kidding, that would never have been me. I was always destined to shake things up, to make waves. It was in my nature.

In that vein, I smiled sweetly and said, "No shoes?"

"You're only getting clothes so you don't mess up my plane," Dagen said, his voice a low snarl. "I don't want you to cream the leather."

The suggestion I might be turned on by him in any way was both laughable and disgusting. At another time I'd make a comment about Ben being hot enough to do that for me, or even one of his goons. I didn't want to draw any further attention to Ben. Nor did I want to give anyone else any ideas.

Instead, I just made a gagging sound and stayed still while two goons reattached themselves to my arms.

I caught sight of Ben, who was now dressed and

looking better for having been healed. He wore a tight fitting black t-shirt which was drawn firmly over his muscular chest, and light grey track pants.

If Asshole chose that outfit to distract me, he almost succeeded. I didn't choose bodyguards for their looks—in fact, Jake vetted most of them—but there was a reason I had a past history with the guy that went beyond trust and into lust. Dark hair, brown eyes and only a smattering of tattoos here and there, he was the definition of tall, dark and smokin' hot.

And yeah, those track pants clearly gave away the other reason for the attraction. He had a cock like a racehorse, but without the excessive speed.

"Get them on the plane," Dagen snapped. "And find Jake Blakesley. Take him to our destination." He frowned at me, then at Ben, as if we were somehow to blame for Jake not being here.

Then I understood. He assumed Jake would be in the Cobra with me. That was a logical assumption. We were usually together, or not far from each other. If he took us both, it would effectively cut the head off the organisation. Of course, there were others who could step up to take our place, but all of that would take time and planning. And maybe some bloodshed.

Thank the gods Jake and I weren't together tonight. He would have battened down all the proverbial hatches by now, and been on high alert for anything suspicious. Not that he wasn't always cautious, but he wouldn't be caught unawares, like I was.

I could kick myself for that, but fuck it. A girl should be able to drive around her own city without getting attacked by a rival. Or anyone else for that matter.

The goons pushed me toward the plane. I considered resisting. Even without shifting, I had the self defence skills to take on two of them. It was the twenty or so others which were the problem. Add to that the fact Dagen was all too happy to break my bones. There was no guarantee he'd keep telling his pet witch to heal them.

Head high, I climbed the steps and into the plane. They shoved me into a seat at the front, and arrayed themselves beside and around me.

More goons shoved Ben up the steps and toward the back of the plane. We exchanged a quick look before he trudged past, looking pissed off, but resigned.

I knew it was too much to ask that we be allowed to sit together, but to make it worse, Dagen slipped into the seat directly behind me. As if the stink wasn't bad enough. Shame to ruin a perfectly good plane with the smell of black wolf.

Fortunately, it was offset by the scent of two white wolves.

Make that three. I forced my expression to remain neutral when Hutton stepped inside the plane. I hadn't seen him outside, so either he just arrived, or he was behind the tinted windows of a car.

His nostrils flared, but he didn't even glance my way. He kept going past and headed to the rear of the aircraft.

I barely gave him more than a flick of my eyes before my gaze slid away. I knew Jake didn't trust him, but we'd sent him to work for Dagen to find out what he was up to. That was still his job, as far as I was concerned. If he wasn't on our side, I'd find out soon enough. If he was, then he could report back to Jake, whether or not I made it out of here in one piece. Hopefully he was smarter than to try to rescue me, or anything stupid like that. All that would do was blow his cover and get him killed.

I might be *the* Ivory but this whole thing was bigger than me. People's lives depended on Ivory Claw. Their livelihoods too. I hadn't spent years building it up only for my own benefit. I mean, that didn't hurt, but that wasn't my sole motivation.

The moment the plane door closed, I felt like they'd cut off my air supply. It was immediately harder to breathe. More difficult still when every breath brought the smell of testosterone, black leather and jet fuel. A heady combination under other circumstances. The scent of filthy rich men and their minions.

In this case, a filthy rich man whose parents killed mine. Whose parents I killed in retaliation. A man who wanted everything I had, and was apparently done waiting to make a grab for it.

He leaned forward and his breath grazed my neck. I cursed myself for putting my hair up and leaving my throat exposed.

"Sit back and enjoy the ride," he said, his voice low and menacing. "The fun and games are just beginning." He brushed the back of his hand over the bruises on my cheek.

"Shouldn't you be buckled up?" I asked. "I'd hate it if we hit turbulence and you got hurt. On second thought, don't buckle up." I twisted around just far enough to give him a sweet, sarcastic smile.

He turned his hand and wound it around my neck. He squeezed, pressing his fingers into my skin.

I responded with a stare of pure ice. If he thought he'd scare me with a threat of strangulation, he'd have to think again. I wasn't afraid of much, and certainly not of dying. It would be inconvenient, but not the fear it was for most people. I'd seen so much of it, I was desensitised by now.

He squeezed tighter, obviously annoyed at my lack of reaction, but he hadn't done all of this just to kill me in a fit of irritation. He waited until my vision started to blur, then released and pushed me away.

"Ice Bitch, I'm going to have fun with you." His smile was chilling.

"I can't wait." I sat back around, checked my seatbelt and thought up ways I was going to make him pay for this. I made a mental list I could check off later, one by one. By the time I was done, he'd wish he never took his first breath.

The engine turned over and the plane started to taxi toward the runway.

2

I DIDN'T REALISE until the plane lifted off that I hoped we'd go south. I knew people there, in several locations. People Jake would contact first.

My heart sank as the plane rose and headed north.

I recalled that Dagen had properties on the north coast. Hells, so did I, for that matter. Mostly rental properties with perfectly ordinary people living in them. They didn't much care who owned them, as long as they had a place to live, and the rent didn't go up too often.

Whatever, they weren't people who could help me.

"Nice view, isn't it?" Dagen asked.

Without thinking, I glanced out the window.

*Fucker.*

He made sure we passed right over the top of Crimson on the way. From here, it just looked like a tall building with a helipad on top. Not much different to a dozen other buildings in the area. I half expected it to explode after we flew past, but it didn't.

I knew very well that dear, old Asshole wanted to own the place. Blowing it up would be dumb, even for him. Still, I wouldn't put it past him, just to see the look on my face.

"It's okay." I squinted, but of course Jake didn't appear on the helipad with a bazooka, or even a dragon, to knock the plane out of the sky. He and Cooper were down there somewhere, worrying. I could feel it.

Or maybe I was projecting my own emotions. I was as worried about them as I was about myself. Maybe more so. Not because they couldn't take care of themselves, and each other, but because Dagen was a motherfucker who held a grudge against them both as well as me. Jake more than Cooper, but anyone involved with me was automatically Dagen's enemy. Anyone involved with him was mine. Anyone but Hutton, until I knew for sure where he stood.

We reached cruising altitude out over the ocean and the goon beside me unbuckled his seatbelt.

I kept mine on. There was still time for the guys to send a dragon shifter after us. Maybe a phoenix. We had both on the payroll. Failing that, lighting might appear out of a perfectly clear sky and strike us.

None of that happened. Dagen's men moved around the plane, talking in low voices and giving me open glances. Some of them looked uneasy, but most looked triumphant, like outnumbering Ben and I and sticking us on a plane somehow meant they won.

The one or two who dared to catch my eye got an icy gaze in return. They all blinked first, then turned away.

*That's right, bastards,* I thought. *I'm not beaten yet. Even after my heart stops, my legacy will fight on. And my guys.*

I itched to look back and check on Ben, but forced myself to keep my eyes forward. My senses were open to the smells around me: anxiety, fear, indifference. Smug-as-fuck, that was Dagen. I didn't get any indication that anyone planned anything. Rather, I felt like everyone was waiting, anticipating whatever Asshole had planned for Ben and me. Or me, at least. I wasn't sure Ben registered on their radars. Good. I would do what I could to be sure it stayed that way.

"It won't be long now," Alistair said in my ear.

Fuck, I hadn't noticed him leaning forward again, but there he was, his breath on my neck again.

"Has it ever been long?" I asked sweetly. "You seem like the sort of man who has to overcompensate in other areas. This plane, for example." I gestured around me. It was actually smaller than my jet, but I couldn't resist taking a dig at the size of his cock.

He chuckled. "It's long enough and thick enough to break you in two, bitch."

"Don't call me bitch," I said over my shoulder. I braced myself for him to strike me, or try to choke me again. Something.

He chuckled again. "I give you full points for trying to pretend you haven't lost. Or maybe you aren't ready to accept it. But you will. Everything you have is mine now. Or will be soon." He slid his fingers along the side of my neck.

I shivered involuntarily. If I didn't know vampires weren't real, I'd start to wonder about him. He was creepy, liked black suits and seemed to be obsessed with my neck. Was there a word for that? I knew it wasn't neck-rophilia, but the thought made the sides of my mouth twitch.

"Dream on," I told him. "Nothing of mine will ever be yours. Jake will make sure of that."

Dagen snorted and let his fingertips rest against the pulse point at my throat. "There's nothing your lapdog can do now. In a couple of days, he'll be dead. Along with that boytoy of yours. Wheeler's nephew. He's as good as dead. I have no use for him."

I pretended to yawn. I really wanted to jerk away from his touch, but I wouldn't give him the satisfaction of knowing he creeped me out.

"Do we get a meal on this flight?" I asked. "Or a movie? The service on board sucks."

"How about I shove my cock down your throat?" he said. "That should fill you up."

"I said meal, not a tiny bag of nuts," I retorted. I was gagging at the idea of his cock anywhere near my mouth. And bracing myself for him to hit me. For some reason, even nice guys didn't like it when you said their dick was small.

His fingers dug into my skin, just above the collar. "You think you're so, fucking clever, don't you? You will regret every single word that comes out of your mouth." He slid his fingers around, worked them under the back of the collar and yanked it back so hard I gagged as it dug into my throat.

"You're my pet, bitch. You will learn to behave," he hissed. "I am your master now. Get used to being on your knees."

I struggled to breathe, much less think up a good comeback to that. I leaned back to take some of the pressure off, but he tugged harder.

My vision started to blur. My head swam. I reached up and tried to hook my fingers around the collar, to pull it away from my throat. I struggled to draw a breath, even half a breath.

He shoved me away and the pressure was gone.

I coughed and sucked in a few, frantic breaths before I managed to regain my composure.

"You see, bitch?" He gloated like the fucking prick he was. "It's so easy to take everything from you. I can do it with one hand."

"I'm sure your hand gets a workout," I said between coughs.

"Thinking of things I'm going to do with you, it did," he agreed. "But now I have your mouth, I can give it a rest."

"If you put any body part near my mouth, I'll bite it off," I said evenly. I rubbed my throat and winced. The skin already felt bruised. "I need to pee," I said after a moment. "Please tell me this toy of yours has a toilet."

I glanced back between the gap in the seats as Asshole nodded at one of his henchmen.

"Leave the door open and watch her."

"You're not going to watch me yourself?" I asked. That seemed like something he'd get off on.

He ignored me.

Spoilsport.

The goon beside me reached for my seatbelt and unclicked it before pulling me to my feet and ushering me to the rear of the plane.

I didn't dare to glance at Ben as I walked past, but I saw he was alive. For now. I managed a tight half smile that he may or may not have seen, and shuffled past.

Hutton sat on the other side, a couple of rows back. He didn't look my way either.

The toilet was nothing to write home about, but moving around the plane gave me the chance for a good look. Slightly smaller than mine, it was fitted out to carry people, not be luxurious. It had no couches, no room in the back for a bed, no bar. None of the fun things.

"I won't tell if you turn your back," I said to the henchman.

He seemed unimpressed. "Hurry up, or I'll help you. I'm sure the boss won't mind."

I was almost certain the boss *would* mind. Dagen seemed like the kind of prick who didn't share his toys until they were broken and chewed. Unless he got something out of it.

I rolled my eyes and did what I needed to do as quickly as I could, glad the t-shirt was long enough to fall almost to my knees. If the goon thought he'd see anything, he'd be mistaken. Still, the lack of privacy was discomfiting, bordering on humiliating. Which was the point. They were trying to get to me. They'd have to try harder than that.

I stepped out of the tiny cubicle—without stealing anything, or ripping off the toilet seat, how amazing is that—to the murmur of hushed, concerned voices and the sound of a soft alarm from the direction of the cockpit.

I laughed softly. "That would be about bloody right. I get dragged aboard Dagen's fucking jet and then it crashes into the ocean. This is the most Mondayish Thursday I've had in a long time."

"It's Wednesday," the goon said.

"That figures." I shrugged. "Wednesdays are often disappointing. I was born on one."

"Quiet," the goon snapped.

I decided he looked like an Eric. He had a long face and a chin like a slide. His nose was also long and his eyes too close together.

He grabbed my arm and shoved me back toward my seat.

The beeping increased. I was no expert, but it sounded like a fuel warning. Or someone put their seat back too far and bumped someone else's knees. People on planes were so inconsiderate.

I added Eric to the list when he shoved me faster.

"Hurry up, bitch," he growled. He must have been taking etiquette lessons from Alistair.

"Don't call me bitch," I growled back.

Eric's face turned pink. I was almost certain he'd hit me if he had permission to.

"Bitch is appropriate," he said instead. "You murdered my parents and grandparents. If the boss let me, I'd open the door and throw you out."

I rolled my eyes. "Take it up with the boss. His family started the killing."

"You kept it going," Eric pointed out. "You could have just done as you were all told. Stayed out of the way. We could all have lived our lives."

"I have two words for you," I told him. I frowned. "Wait, is brainwashing one word or two? Whatever. What the Dagens did was little better than genocide. We weren't going to take that lying down."

Eric shoved me back toward my seat.

I half fell over both of them before I managed to scramble back and grab both sides of my seatbelt.

Dagen wasn't in his seat, he must be in the cockpit. How appropriate.

Eric looked down on me with eyes laced with barely contained fury. I had no doubt in my mind that if we weren't on a plane full of people, and if he wouldn't get in major trouble for it, he would take out his frustrations on me. Whether that would be with his fists or his cock, I don't know. Maybe both.

I clicked my seatbelt and tried not to appear rattled. It was easy enough to think Alistair Dagen was the enemy here, and he was. But I was also surrounded by men who hated me as deeply as I hated them. Men who were bigger and stronger than I was, especially if they worked together.

Eric flopped down beside me and placed his hands in his lap, over his dick.

Yeah, I figured that might be his weapon of choice.

I gave him a long look. "You'd regret it."

He shrugged one shoulder. "Maybe. Maybe not. Might be worth it at the time."

"Yeah, but for how long after that? Until your boss cuts your throat? Where is that going to get you? Just dead, that's where."

He shrugged. "Dead, but vindicated."

"Right, then." I couldn't even claim it was the first time I talked to a man so casually about my own potential rape. If it wasn't for Jake, that would have been my fate years ago.

I was acutely aware he wasn't here right now.

"So, is the plane going to crash?" I looked between the seats in front of me, but the cockpit door was closed.

"I don't know," he admitted. "If I'm going to die anyway…"

I actually laughed. "Dude, if you can do it before we hit the water, then I'm not your problem."

He smirked.

Before he could speak, the plane shuddered.

"This wasn't how I imagined dying." I sighed. "What's your name?"

He glanced over at me. "Huh?"

"If we're going to die together, I figured I should know your name." I winced when the plane shuddered again. "Is it Eric?"

"What? No. It's Toby. Tobias." He looked back over his shoulder at something.

"What is it?" I asked. "Dragon? Phoenix? Pterodactyl?"

"I dunno, I can't see," he said. His head snapped back toward me. "Did you do something?"

The question took me by surprise, but then I laughed. "Yes, absolutely. I'm sitting inside the plane, while trying to make it crash so I die too."

Thankfully he had at least a basic understanding of sarcasm.

"If you're going to die, you'll want to take as many of us with you as you can," he said.

I smiled. "Well, yes. A queen needs servants in the afterlife." I rolled my eyes. "Whatever is going on, it's not me. Your boss probably skimped on the cost of maintenance. Or he has other enemies, apart from me. I mean, not everyone looks favourably on the days of Dagen rule over the state."

After a moment, I added, "Tobias, are you in on an assassination attempt? I'd think better of you if you were."

"Fuck off," he snarled. "I'm loyal. The only person I'd assassinate is you."

"That's very touching." I looked back through the plane. I couldn't see Hutton, but I met Ben's eyes. Electricity zapped between us. If I was going to die, I'd rather be in his arms than here with Toby.

I wanted to get up and stagger through the plane to him. I would find Hutton, and the three white wolves could huddle together and wait it out.

But if we didn't crash, we would have shown all our cards. *I* would have. Revealed that I had feelings for Ben, and that Hutton sort of worked for me. I couldn't rule out the possibility that this was some kind of twisted trick.

When the fuck did I get so cynical? Oh yeah, when I came home from school to a home decorated with my parent's blood.

Wonderful. I would die alone because I was suspicious of everyone's motives. Yeah, well, it kept me alive for this long.

"So, Toby Tobias. Does this plane have parachutes? No? Oxygen masks? Airbags?"

"Barfbags." He nodded to the pocket in the seat in front of him.

"For the record, Dagen being a tightass is going to kill us all." The plane shuddered harder this time. It dropped for a good two seconds. My stomach flew up into my throat.

"Too late for a fuck?" Toby asked. He almost smiled. Almost.

"Good to see you have a sense of humour," I said

dryly. "I think we have time for me to blow you a kiss."

He sighed. "Can you blow my cock? Even if I don't finish, I could die kinda happy."

"You can shift and suck it yourself," I pointed out.

"No wonder we all hate you," he said. But I had a feeling he didn't hate me anymore. Funny how seeing a monster as a real person makes them seem like less of a monster.

I laughed softly. "Nothing worse than a woman who won't put out," I said sarcastically.

I groaned as the plane dropped again. I might need that barfbag yet.

"For what it's worth," I said slowly, "I know how you feel. We're people who got caught up in shit. Then we kept on with the shit. I was hoping it would end with me."

"It still might," he said from behind clenched teeth.

"Dagen and I die, it won't end this," I said. "If anything, it'll make it worse." At least he'd be dead. That was a plus.

So would I, that was a minus.

"Nothing will end this while both sides are left," Toby said.

That was an oversimplification, but he might not be wrong.

"Yeah, but I couldn't bring myself to kill all of you." I glanced over at him. "My bad, I guess."

It might not be a mistake I made again, assuming I got out of this alive. Shame, he was tolerable, if you can get past the whole temptation-to-rape me thing. That was a big hurdle.

"Yeah, your bad." He smiled at me, but his eyes betrayed his terror. He signed up to die for Dagen, if he had to, but not like this.

"I hope you can float," I told him.

He sighed. "I can't even swim."

The plane dropped again.

"Well, fuck," I said softly.

"Yeah, well fuck. Dagen is a shitty boss anyway."

I laughed, low and husky. "You better hope to die if you're going to say that out loud." I wasn't going to give up until I was done. "Can you take this collar off me? I'd feel better if I could doggie paddle."

"It needs magic for that," Toby said. "I don't have any." Was that actual regret in his eyes?

"Figures." I closed my eyes when the plane shuddered and dropped. "Worst ride ever."

Toby snorted. "Yeah."

The alarm got louder as the plane headed downward.

3

I squeezed my eyes shut until I realised the plane levelled off. The alarm still sounded, but softer now. We banked steeply and headed in a north-westerly direction.

I leaned over and spoke softly in Toby's ear. "I won't tell anyone you said he was a shitty boss." I patted his arm for good measure. It didn't hurt to try to make allies, even amongst the enemy. Especially amongst the enemy.

"I...only said that because I thought I was going to die." Was he pissed off at me, himself or both?

"You will die if he knows you said that." I was guessing. Dagen was petty but was he that petty? If I had to guess, I would say yes, yes he was.

From the expression on Toby's face, I was right.

"He won't hear it from me," I said. "Promise." I made no guarantees about the people around us having overheard. That was his problem. I also wouldn't guarantee I wouldn't tell someone and have them tell Dagen. That would depend on how he treated me from now on. If he tried anything, I would make absolutely certain Dagen knew about it. I knew he knew that too.

Yes, I could also be petty.

"I presume we're not far from our destination." I peered out the window.

Toby grunted. He was back in full grumpy goon mode. I sensed I wouldn't get anything else out of him. That was fine. I didn't want to be his friend, and I didn't want to risk lowering my guard. He was the enemy. As if I could forget for a moment.

The alarm pinged as we passed low over a town on the north coast. Onyx Head, unless I missed my guess. Where else would black wolves hang out? It was one of those sleepy towns that got trendy and expensive with the injection of cash from people like Dagen. It was probably full of movie stars and drugs or some shit. Cooper would probably love it. Jake would tell them all to get fucked and go surfing. He was a pretty good surfer when he got the chance to get out in the water.

As for me, my skin burned just thinking about going out in the sun.

The alarm was still pinging as we headed towards a small runway. Not surprisingly, a fire truck waited beside it. Presumably that was just a precaution. They didn't actually think we were going to burst into flames on landing. Right?

The wheels hit the runway with barely a bounce, but we flew along so fast I thought we would take off at the other end. Of course, we didn't. The plane slowed and turned to taxi back along the runway and towards the small airport.

"Well, we survived that in one piece," I remarked under my breath. Was that a good thing though, or a terrible thing?

The plane came to a stop and the goons hurried to get the door open and the steps out. Dagen emerged from the cockpit looking slightly pale. He was the first one off the aircraft.

Like a rat deserting a sinking ship.

Toby unbuckled his seatbelt and nodded for me to do the same.

I was tempted to thank him sarcastically, but I decided not to screw with our uneasy peace. Instead, I unclicked and even stood without being asked, or dragged to my feet. That didn't stop Toby from grabbing my arm and pushing me to, and then out, the door.

I managed to look dignified when I stepped out in the breeze of what was now mid-morning.

"I hope you fire whoever is supposed to maintain that for you." I jerked my head back toward the plane and gave Asshole an insincere smile.

"I'll have them killed," he growled.

I couldn't even call him excessive, it's exactly what I would do. Anyone who risked my life like that forfeited theirs. Especially if they cut corners.

"Get the bitch to the car," he snapped. His mood was worse than before. Bad enough to put me on edge.

He watched me through narrowed eyes, clearly expecting me to remind him not to call me that.

I wasn't scared of him, but I wasn't stupid. I could tell he was hoping I'd give him an excuse to break my other cheekbone. Or just kill me outright.

"Come on." Toby shoved me over to one of the waiting cars. Not a black SUV, to my surprise. Rather, it was an ordinary, black sedan.

No four wheel driving for us today. Shame, that might have been fun.

Toby opened the door and let me climb in without help.

Before he could follow me inside, Dagen snapped, "Not you. I can see on your face she got to you already." He nodded to another of his men. "Terminate him. You two, stay close to her."

Toby looked shocked, but they dragged him away before I could react, or respond.

Dagen was more astute than I gave him credit for. And a *really* shitty boss.

I sat back and watched out the tinted windows while the henchmen took Ben to another car.

Hutton followed the goons who were dragging a white faced Toby to yet another car. I wasn't sure if I should curse his name or not. I didn't want Toby dead because of me, but he was still one of Dagen's men, more or less. If Hutton exposed himself in some attempt to save Toby…

I ducked my head. There was nothing I could do or say that would change anything now. For all I knew, Hutton would be the one to kill him. I hated not being certain which side the man was on. Just because he made it clear he wanted to fuck me didn't mean he wasn't ready to strangle me.

I had that effect on some people. I have no idea why.

Much to my joy, Dagen climbed into the front

passenger seat of the car and we pulled away from the airport.

This whole exercise must be costing him a fortune. Between the men, the cars and the plane, I'd conservatively guess half a million dollars. I'm not saying I'm not worth it, but I would have done it on a much more conservative budget. Or just killed him and not bothered with all the bullshit at all. Lucky for me, his approach was different to mine.

We slipped out of the carpark and onto the coastal highway. Traffic was light at this time of morning. Lucky, because a parade of dark coloured cars would get noticed in a place like this. They might think I'm a movie star, or a rock star. I mean, I *am* a rock star, but I can't sing for shit. Ask Jake, he says I howl. So does he, if we're honest.

Fuck, I already missed him so much it hurt. Cooper too. I should be having breakfast right now and arguing with Jake because I want to eat some sugary crap, when all he lets me eat is healthy stuff. Why do I let him tell me what to eat? It's just a part of who we are. Like an old married couple. If I really wanted to eat cake for breakfast, I would do it. I didn't really want it, but I liked to pretend I did.

Okay, sometimes I did actually want cake. The

point was, it was like a running joke between us that most people wouldn't understand.

I forced my head back up. I had to pay attention to where we were going. I had to keep an eye out for a chance to get the hells out of this situation. If I ran, I needed to know which way to head.

We turned up a private road with the bush heavy on either side. Bush a person could get lost in, if they could cover their scent.

We slowed and passed through a heavy gate. The fence disappeared into the brush on either side, but it was tall and solid. Not insurmountable. I hoped.

I glanced back to see the gate swing shut behind the last car.

When I turned back, Dagen twisted around his seat, watching me, his eyes triumphant.

I flipped him off. I wasn't beaten yet.

He turned back as we drove out of the brush and past a wide expanse of lawn. In the middle of that was a predictably huge house, with a multi-car garage attached to the side.

The driver slid the car into a space near the middle and killed the engine.

"Home, sweet home," Dagen said lightly.

It must be a recent purchase, because I didn't recall his parents owning anything like this. If they did, I would have taken it and used it. It looked like a nice little bolt hole.

"Get the bitch out of the car," he ordered. "Bring her out to the lawn."

Once again, goons gripped my arms and led me out of the garage and into the sun.

I blinked and squinted against the glare. It was bright out from behind tinted windows, but it was pretty here. And quiet. I reassessed my thoughts about this being a nice place to stay. The lack of city noise would drive me crazy in a day or two.

The goons led me across the grass to a small shed.

"Guest accommodation?" I guessed.

They didn't say anything, they just walked me inside.

Dagen followed a moment later. "I have something for you, pet."

"No thanks," I said immediately. Unless it was my freedom, I wanted nothing from him.

His men walked Ben in and my heart stopped. For a long moment, I thought his present would be to kill Ben. I definitely didn't want that, if that was his idea of a gift.

"Shackle him over there," Dagen ordered. He nodded toward one of several sets of restraints attached to the wall. Either he planned this for a while, or this was just a regular day in the life of the sadistic asshole. My bet was on both.

"And you," Dagen said to me, "can bathe first. I don't like dirty pets in my house."

For the first time, I noticed a bath in the corner of the building. It was full of water that looked clear, but cold.

"I prefer showers," I said.

"Strip her," Dagen said softly.

Oh yeah, he was absolutely living out some kind of dark fantasy right here.

"I can take my own clothes off," I said coldly.

Either they didn't hear or they didn't give a shit. While two men held my arms, another tore the t-shirt off my body, ripping the fabric in two. He tossed the shirt aside and slid his hands into the sides of my track pants, against my skin, before pushing those down to my feet.

The assholes on my arms jerked me forward, forcing me to step out of the pants.

I didn't need to look to see the erections. The smell of arousal filled the room like stale heat.

I caught Ben's expression. He pulled against the shackles, obviously ready to rip off some heads.

I shook mine. There was no point in him getting killed, not over this.

"Get in the bath." Dagen's voice was rough. He made no attempt to hide the tent in his pants.

I contained a shudder and stepped into the icy water. My skin pebbled before I even sank down to my ass. It was fucking cold, but it provided some illusion that I was covered.

"There's soap and shampoo." Dagen crossed his arms over his chest and watched.

I followed his gaze and snorted. Dog shampoo. The man was a fucking hypocrite. As if he wasn't also a wolf.

"I prefer people shampoo," I said.

"Use that, or I'll wash you myself," he snapped.

Ugh, hard pass. I picked up the shampoo and poured some onto my hand. It smelled nice at least, like vanilla. It probably kept away fleas too. Bonus.

"This would be more fun if I had a squeaky toy to play with," I remarked. I placed a hand on my head and let the shampoo trickle down before I started to lather.

"You'll have a bone to play with soon enough," he said.

By now, at least a dozen of his men stood inside

the shed, watching me wash myself in a bath meant for a pet dog.

I tried to pretend I didn't care. That I didn't care who saw when my breasts rose above the water as I lay back to rinse. I tried not to think about what every man dressed in a black suit would do to me, given the chance.

A sliver of fear and humiliation crept under my skin and took hold. I had worked hard for so many years to make sure I was never treated like this again. I surrounded myself with people who respected me, feared me.

Here, I felt stripped back, beyond just my clothes. Vulnerable. Worse still when I recalled how little it took for him to bring me down to this.

*Toughen up,* I told myself. *You've gone through worse. You'll get through this.*

I soaped and rinsed quickly, then climbed out of the water before anyone could 'help' me.

I shivered, not just with cold. I stood in front of so many men, dripping like a wet dog.

"Here." Dagen grabbed a towel from a nearby shelf—clean by the look of it—and stepped almost close enough to hand it to me.

I would have to move toward him to take it. The

expression on his face sent chills down my spine and froze me to the spot.

"Well?" he demanded.

I wanted the relative, false safety of the towel wrapped around myself, but I couldn't bring myself to move. Everything in me was screaming at me not to get any closer to him.

Ben sensed it too. In my peripheral vision, I saw him strain against the shackles.

Dagen lowered his hand and took the handful of steps to me.

Unable to stop myself, I took a couple back.

He smiled. If you can call lips turning up on the sides, combined with a sneer, a smile.

He gave the faintest of nods and I was surrounded by three henchmen. Assholes. *Hench-holes.* Two took my arms, another stood behind me.

"I tried to be hospitable," Dagen said slowly.

Without meaning to, I snorted. If this was hospitable, I hated to see how he treated people he really didn't like.

Dagen's body stiffened and his mouth twisted into a slanted scowl. He snarled. *"Enough of this shit."*

He backhanded me across the same cheek he left bruises on a few hours earlier.

The blow was so hard, I was knocked back a step. Searing pain bloomed in my cheek.

Later, I wouldn't remember if I fell, or was pushed by his henchholes. Either way, I landed heavily on my knees on the hard floor. I tried to stagger back to my feet, but all three of them held me in place. One on each shoulder, the other with his hands on the sides of my neck. His fingertips brushed my throat.

I forced myself to breathe. Panic rose inside me. Blind fear that made thinking hard, like it used to when I was a kid. An orphan. My heart raced so hard it might stop from the effort. Panic threatened to swamp me, drag me down into the darkest places I thought I left behind, in the past.

I held back anything more than a wince of pain, and the sob of fear that threatened to escape my lips. I kept my eyes on the ground for a good couple of minutes.

*It was okay. I was okay. I was alive.*

Whatever happened now, I could deal with. I told myself all of that and more, but I wasn't sure I believed it, deep down.

When I looked back up, Dagen stood in front of me. The look he gave me sent the coldest shivers through my spine. I had absolutely no doubt in my mind what he intended.

I swallowed and shook my head. "No," I whispered. Every centimetre of me trembled.

He unzipped his pants to expose his erection.

Shit.

No.

*No.*

*Nope.*

I shook my head vigorously, and writhed and struggled with everything I had.

In the back of my mind, I acknowledged Ben's shouts of outrage and despair. He was as powerless to help me as I was.

Three men held my head still while Dagen shoved his cock between my lips. He rammed it all the way to the back of my throat until I gagged.

"Take it all, bitch," he growled.

I wanted to bite, but he slammed into me again and again. All I could do was keep breathing and not literally choke on his cock.

I fought against the hands that held me, but their grip was tight. I thought I knew how it felt to be vulnerable. Until now. This was the first time in my entire life I felt totally, absolutely, utterly powerless. I wanted to crawl back into the bath. I wanted to stand in front of them dripping wet and naked. I could take all the humiliation they had to give. Anything but *this*.

"Fuck, yes," Asshole muttered. "That shut the bitch up."

The other assholes, the ones holding me so their coward of a boss could rape my mouth, actually laughed. *Shitheads.*

Tears poured down my cheeks. As they dripped off my chin, a tiny part of me hardened, like a callous over my heart. I would survive this. I would make every last one of them pay. They would live to regret having touched me and then they would die.

His pounding slowed, his breathing became more ragged.

I gagged. *Gods, no.*

A moment later, he shuddered, rammed his cock as far down my throat as he could and came.

Hot cum squirted into my mouth. I wanted to spit, to throw up. Die. Something.

*Anything.*

"Come on, bitch," he grunted.

I tried not to. I shook my head, but they held me fast. His cock was still deep. I had no choice but to give in to reflex and swallow. The taste was sour, like lemon juice dosed with salt. I immediately wanted to throw it back up onto his feet. Or onto the bastards that held me down. They were a bunch of fucking cowards, all of them. Four men against one woman who was smaller than any of them.

"There we go, that wasn't so hard, was it?" he asked. "Good girl." He actually patted my head before he slid out of me and left me gasping on the floor.

I managed to spit a couple of times, but my mouth was already dry.

"I'd call her first lesson a success. Bring her inside." He zipped up his pants like nothing happened, and walked away.

I was dragged to my feet and hauled toward the main house. Ben was unshackled and pulled along behind me. I knew I didn't imagine the streaks of tears on his cheeks too, the fury in his eyes. He would tear them to shreds the second he got the chance.

*Hold on to that anger,* I thought. *You're going to need it.*

Gods, I could use a mint right about now. Or better yet, toothpaste and a stiff toothbrush. Even better than that, Jake at the gates with an army.

Right now, I couldn't throw off the feeling help wasn't going to come, even from within myself.

4

I THOUGHT they might take me back to the garage, or a dog kennel. I wouldn't have put it past Asshole, and right now I didn't care. I just wanted to curl up in a ball and try to pretend what just happened, hadn't. Maybe cry for a while before I think of ways to carve him up with a blunt, rusty tool of some kind.

I was led straight past the garage and into the main house, across expensive hardwood floors and up stairs covered in thick, plush carpet.

To my surprise, everything was tastefully decorated. I expected tacky wallpaper with giant flamingos on it. Or for everything to be black. I would bet a million dollars Alistair Dagen hadn't decorated the place himself. Everything from the finishings, to the placement of the furniture looked staged, like an expert arranged everything carefully.

Even the art on the walls looked impersonal, except for a few Dagen family photographs here and there. Not one of them showed a hint of a smile. In spite of him claiming he wanted revenge for their deaths, there didn't seem to have been much love lost between Alastair Dagen and his parents. Fair enough, they were all jerks.

"I was going to accommodate you in the bath-house," Dagen said. "But I thought you might prefer some creature comforts. Consider it a taste of the way you could live if you behave yourself."

I didn't even roll my eyes. For one thing, it would hurt my face. For another, I refused to give him an excuse to touch me again. Instead, I forced my expression into one of icy serenity and kept it there like a steel facade. I was ashamed of myself for letting my mask crack. That couldn't happen again. He got off on getting to me and I couldn't give him the satisfaction.

*I wouldn't.*

One of the goons opened the door and stepped aside. Ben and I were pushed into a room which was nothing short of luxurious. It was the kind of space that would look right at home in my house. Well, almost. I wouldn't have chosen those gold doorknobs on what I assumed was the bathroom door. I also wouldn't have chosen quite that shade of grey for the carpet.

"You'll notice there are two bedrooms in your suite," Dagen said as though offering some kind of gift. "I thought you might appreciate your privacy. Unfortunately, you will have to share the bathroom. But there is hot water. I'm sure you'd like to wash the dirt off your *knees*."

He sounded so fucking smug. I wanted to push him out the window.

Ben looked at Dagen, then at me. He swallowed and looked like he was barely able to contain himself. His hands were curled into fists.

I shook my head. As tempting as it was to let him take a swing at Dagen, there was no point risking him getting killed for it.

"In case you're wondering, the window doesn't open," Dagen said. "And of course there will be guards on the door. A meal will be brought to you in an hour. And yes, there are cameras and microphones all through the room. Just in case you decide to try to plot your escape. There's no way out."

If he didn't think I would take that as a challenge,

he had another thought coming. But he knew that, I saw it on his face. His smug, hateful face.

He ignored Ben, but patted my cheek before he turned and left.

The door clicked shut behind him.

Ben exhaled loudly and reached out a hand toward me. "Ivory—"

I shook my head and held myself out of reach. "I'm okay," I lied. I turned away and hurried into the bathroom. I didn't want to see the pity on his face. I couldn't deal with that right now. Holding myself together was difficult enough.

I caught my reflection in the mirror. One side of my face was black and purple with bruises. In contrast, the other side was starkly white, even for me.

Barely containing a sob, I dropped to my chafed, sore knees beside the toilet and threw up everything in my stomach. It wasn't much. I tried not to think about what it actually was. I was just relieved to have it out of me.

At some point, Ben crouched beside me and held my hair off my face. He lightly rubbed my back with one hand. Somehow, he even managed to snag a towel and wrap it around me.

"This is bullshit," he said, mimicking my thoughts exactly. "You deserve better than this."

I spat a couple of times, then sat on the cold floor and exhaled. "Do I? I've done some pretty shitty things in my life. Maybe this is what I get for all of it."

One side of his mouth drew up. "You don't believe that," he said. "I don't."

"You sound like Jake," I said.

He managed a smile, albeit faint and watery. "Thank you."

I rolled my eyes, then winced. I was right, it did hurt. "Are you sure it's a compliment?"

"Absolutely," he agreed. "Jake is a legend. Almost as much as you are."

I tucked my legs close to myself. "I don't feel like much of a legend right now." I felt like a rag doll who got left behind by the side of the road in the rain.

"Do you want to have a shower?" He stood and turned on the water. "It's actually warm. And there's proper shampoo, and body wash." He picked up a bottle and took a sniff. "Okay, I was half expecting that to be full of piss, but it smells all right."

I grimaced. "Don't give him any ideas." I would absolutely not be surprised if he had them switched out in an hour or two.

"Sorry." Ben put the shampoo bottle back. "I had a peek in the wardrobe. There's even clothes in there for us. They look like they might fit, more or less. You, anyway. I had a feeling they planned for Jake to be here, not me."

"I think you might be right." I looked around for cameras. It seemed unlikely Dagen would miss the opportunity to watch me have a shower. I couldn't see one, but I knew they were there.

"Do you want to talk about it?" Ben asked softly. "What Dagen did... I mean…"

"Don't," I said. "Don't go there. Don't think about it. I don't want to. It's—" I shook my head. "It's in the past." Yeah, right. As if I wouldn't have nightmares about the way his cock grazed my teeth. About the way he felt. About the way he tasted.

My stomach heaved. I leaned over the toilet bowl and retched, but there was nothing left to throw up.

"Okay," he said gently. "It's forgotten." He sounded compliant, but I wasn't fooled. He wouldn't forget any more than I would. Worse, he would blame himself because he couldn't stop it, even though there was nothing he could do.

I gave him a long, firm look. "Remember, we have to do whatever it takes to survive. No matter what that is. We keep looking for a way out, a gap, a hole, *anything*. In the meantime, we survive. Understood?"

"Understood." He looked like he had more to say, but wasn't sure of the right words. He never was much of a talker. Instead, he gave me a look that spoke more volumes than the National Library. I knew he cared about me, but I didn't know how much until now.

He crouched back down. I managed to keep from flinching when he put a hand on the side of my face that wasn't a mess of bruises.

"It's my job to keep you safe," he said, his voice just above a whisper. "Right now, I'm failing spectacularly at that. I wouldn't blame you if you hate me."

Gods, as if I could ever hate him. He was a rock in the middle of a motherfucking hurricane. He always had been. He was the anchor I needed right now.

"We are outnumbered," I reminded him as gently as I could. "You're not failing at anything. You're keeping me sane." I leaned over and lightly kissed his cheek. Then I remembered the last two things that happened to my mouth, and grimaced.

"Ugh, sorry. I should brush my teeth next time." For an hour or two, until the inside of my mouth was sterile.

He smiled. "It's my job to suffer for you." He looked at me sideways, a hint of something more in his eyes. "What would Jake and Cooper think?"

"They just want me to be happy," I said. Jake knew I had a past with Ben. And he trusted the man. That was everything. As for Cooper, he adored Ben for letting him kill the man who tried to assassinate me. To me, that seemed like a very good reason to like someone.

"Funny." He cocked his head. "That's what I want too. Enjoy your shower. Let me know if you want me to wash your back." He tried to smile, but his expression was as haunted as mine.

I supposed it wasn't easy to watch while being unable to stop what happened. That was the point, of course. It was all about power, and putting us in our place.

I nodded. "Yeah, thanks." What I wanted right now was a few minutes to myself. Although, if Dagen was going to watch, we should give him a show. On the other hand, I did my share of touching another person for a while.

I loved nothing better than a long shower, but this time, the one I took was quick. I washed everywhere, taking special care with my face and my knees. I rinsed my mouth several times. It would never get the taste out of my memory. On the day I died I would remember. My stomach turned again.

When I stepped out of the bathroom with a towel wrapped around my body and another round my hair, I smelled the evidence that Asshole actually followed through with his promise of food.

"Is that…bacon?" Maybe I misjudged his evil just a little bit.

"Yeah, but it's undercooked," Ben said.

Or maybe he was as evil as I thought.

Before I ate, I stepped into the wardrobe and rifled through the clothes. Most of it looked like things I would wear: dark skirts, white or red blouses, even heels. A shelf contained several different sizes of underwear. The fact he didn't know what size I wore was perversely satisfying. Clearly he hadn't broken into my house and gone through my underwear drawer. That was good to know. No, it was *really* good to know. It meant his creep factor was ninety-nine point nine percent, rather than one hundred percent. A small but significant difference.

It didn't make him any less of an asshole.

There was even a box of makeup tucked away in a corner. Rude. What made him think I wore makeup?

I opened the lids of a few of the pallets of eyeshadow, and tested the mascara. None of it was my preferred brand, but it would do.

By the time I stepped out of the wardrobe, I was looking and feeling myself again. For now.

"Did you leave me anything?" I asked.

Ben paused with his fork half way to his mouth. He glanced down at his plate, then back at me before he realised I was teasing.

"I left plenty," he said before he shoved his fork into his mouth. "I tasted a bit of everything. Just to make sure it was safe to eat."

I slipped into a chair. "That's good thinking. Unless you died."

"At least we wouldn't both be dead," he pointed out. He didn't seem the slightest bit concerned at the idea of eating poisoned food to save me. I guess that was the job he signed up for as my bodyguard.

Still, with this—whatever this seemed to be growing between us—I wasn't sure how I felt about him risking himself. Losing bodyguards was part of the job. Losing people I cared about…not so much. Under the circumstances, it might be safer not to care. As if I could switch that on and off like a tap.

I grabbed two slices of bread and put bacon, cheese and all the greens onto my sandwich. Jake would almost approve. I thought about taking off the bacon, but he wasn't here to see it. And, you know, I am actually an adult.

In theory.

In spite of the persistent turning in my stomach, I bit into my sandwich and ate. It would suck if I saw the opportunity to escape, but didn't have the energy to do it.

The moment the food hit my stomach, it wanted to bounce back out again. My hands trembled. I tried to force them to stop. My heart raced, vision blurred. All I could see was his cock in front of my face.

It was suddenly incredibly difficult to breathe.

"Have they cut off the oxygen in here or something?" I tried to sound light, but failed. I wanted to run to the window and suck in a bunch of air. He said it wouldn't open, but I could break it. Maybe a chair through the glass…

"Ivory? Ivory. The air is fine. You just need to breathe." How did Ben sound so calm?

"Look at me," he insisted.

"Who is the boss here?" I managed to say. My heart pounded, but it slowed a tiny bit at the sound of his voice. I looked straight at him and breathed in and out through my nose.

He smiled. "Still you. It looks like bacon doesn't agree with you. I better eat yours." He pretended to reach for it.

At least, I assumed he was pretending, because he seemed relatively attached to his hands.

I slapped one of them lightly. "If you touch my bacon, you won't need to worry about whatever Dagen might do to you," I mock growled.

Instead of stealing my bacon, he put his hand on one of my hands. "Are you okay now? No one will think less of you if you freak out once in a while. I do it too." He looked like patience itself right now. Just like how I *should* look.

"I wouldn't be much of an ice queen if I melt at the first sign of trouble," I said. Okay, being on my knees on the floor, choking on the enemy's cock, was more than the 'first sign of trouble.' It was a traumatic event on par with finding my dead parents in pieces. But I was Ivory. I was carved of ice and pain. I didn't give in. Didn't back down. I lived my life on my terms and no one else's. I would not let Dagen take that away from me.

Not ever.

"You don't always have to be the ice queen," Ben said gently. "You're so much more than that. You're the strongest, smartest woman I've ever met. I'll do whatever it takes to be sure you get out of here."

"You're going to make me blush," I said. It was nice to hear, but I was starting to think I wasn't worthy of any of the guys. Like Dagen's touch tainted me somehow. Or maybe I was just a shitty person to start with.

Ben chuckled and squeezed my hand. "I'm sure you've heard all of this before. And more. You deserve to be told every bit of it." With a grin he added, "Boss."

"You don't have to call me boss," I said. "Unless we're in front of Dagen." If the place was really full of cameras and microphones, then we might as well be in front of him now. We probably said far too much, but it was to late to take it back.

"Or I could come up with my own name for you," he mused. "Cooper calls you Ivory. Jake calls you by your birth name. Maybe I should call you something else."

"As long as it's not ice bitch." I grimaced.

"It wouldn't be 'bitch' anything," he said firmly. "I'll think of something. Maybe Queen of Bacon."

That actually made me laugh, albeit bitterly. "We should be careful. That bacon might not be made out of pig."

Ben pushed his to the side of the plate. "That might be what they do with people who betray Dagen. Or piss him off."

"It could be Toby." I made a face at it. "The guy I sat next to on the plane."

"It sounds like you were sitting next to someone friendlier than mine," Ben said. He poked the bacon with the tip of his finger. "The guy next to me wouldn't even say hello. I mean, whatever. I wasn't there to make friends."

"Are you sure?" I teased. "You might have a future as one of Dagen's goons." As if that would happen.

"Firstly, I have a job," Ben said slowly. "Secondly, nothing bad is going to happen to my boss anytime soon, so I won't need a new job. Third, I have a sense of humour. That seems to be lacking around here. And last, I prefer white shirts to black." A slow smile crept onto his face. "Especially on women. Particularly on you, with a bit of juice mixed in."

"You saw that?" I grimaced. Jake accidentally spilled juice all down the front of me a few days ago. I looked like something out of a wet T-shirt competition. I had to walk through Crimson looking like that too.

"Every bit." He grinned. "There wasn't a person in

the whole place who wasn't looking at and appreciating you."

I cocked my head at him. "I'm starting to think that you're cheekier than I realised."

He thought about that for a moment. "No, I've always been like this. I've just been overshadowed by Jake for so long." His eyes widened. "Shit. I didn't mean I was enjoying any of this. I mean… Fuck."

He closed his eyes and shook his head. "If you feel like stabbing me with a fork right now, go ahead. I won't fight back."

I patted him on the arm. "I don't tend to do my own stabbing. I hire people to do that."

"You want me to stab myself with a fork?" he said. "Because I will. Boss."

I pretended to consider that. "Not today," I said finally. "I admit it has been hard to see you past Jake. And Cooper. I wish we'd done this under completely different circumstances, but here we are. It is what it is. And for the record, I prefer the spork as a weapon of choice." I managed a small smile. I liked Ben. I could see this blossoming into something more.

Ben looked surprised, but grinned. "A spork? Why one of those?"

I shrugged one shoulder. "Because it's unexpected. You would see a fork or knife coming. But a spork looks mostly harmless, until it isn't."

"Like you?" he suggested. "Beautiful and sweet on the outside, deadly as fuck on the inside."

"Exactly," I agreed. "I'm just like a spork. And you know what the best part about them is? After you stab someone with them, you can eat soup." I hoped Dagen was listening. He would probably assume we were talking in code. Nope, it was just silly conversation in the life of Ivory. Something to keep us both sane.

"So... I'm guessing I can't call you spork as a nickname?" Ben asked. He wiggled his brows.

"Oh, gods no." I made a face. "I really would use one on you then. Now, you've been here long enough to have assessed at least fifteen different escape routes, right?"

"Sixteen, if we can get enough grease off the bacon. I think we might have eaten too much of it for that." He looked down at the table and sighed. "I tried the windows when you were in the shower. They're double, maybe triple glazed. Not even a chair is going through those suckers. There's no other doors to the outside. No other internal doors. We could try to break through a wall, but they would probably hear us. The floor is solid. We could pull out a light fitting, but neither of us would fit into the hole. Judging by the distance to the ceiling, and the appearance of the house roof, there isn't much of a roof cavity anyway. Not enough room to crawl through."

He sucked in a frustrated breath through his nose. "The only way in or out is through the door we came in. Judging by the overkill we experienced on our way here, there's probably a small army outside. Our best bet is to wait until he moves us somewhere else and be alert for an opportunity."

I nodded. "That was very thorough. Remind me to give you a pay raise when we get out of here." This was the point where I usually joked about giving blow jobs. Instead I felt the edge of a panic attack again.

Fuck Dagen. I hadn't had a panic attack since I was a kid. I didn't want to start having them now. If I got anywhere near his cock, he would be lucky if I stabbed it with a spork.

I pushed the panic down and finished my sandwich.

It was only a matter of time before Dagen came for us again.

5

THE DOOR CREAKED OPEN.

My first thought upon waking was to make sure the housekeeper oiled the hinges. My second was that I wasn't at home. Or at Crimson. I was at Dagen's country house, lying in a wide bed next to Ben.

I sat up and peered through the room.

With a snap, the lights turned on. I squinted against the sudden glare.

"Wakey wakey." Alistair Dagen's voice was chipper. Of course he was evil. Only an evil person would sound that cheerful before the sun even rose. Amiright?

Ben and I sat up. He placed his hands protectively on my shoulders.

"We're awake," I said. I wanted to tell him to fuck off, but decided on the non-confrontational approach of saying nothing more.

"Is that how you greet your host, bitch?" Dagen snarled. "Looks like you need another lesson. Fortunately, that's what I'm here for. Get up." He crossed his arms over his chest and watched.

If he expected us to be naked under the covers, he would be disappointed. Both of us had slept fully dressed except for shoes. I loved my heels, but not enough to sleep in them. Plus, they're not practical footwear for an escape.

I tried to keep my hands from trembling as I pushed the covers off. I waited for some sign of movement from Dagen. Some suggestion he might step towards me. Push me back on the bed. Get his goons to hold me down again while he forced himself on me. Anything.

He made no move. Instead, he waved in the direction of the door. "Take them downstairs."

No less than six of his men closed in around us. Hands gripped my upper arms like a crab's pincers; firm and painful.

We were marched downstairs like they were taking us to a funeral. Maybe they were. Ours.

I doubted it though. Dagen went to a lot of effort,

why would he kill us now? I mean, it might make sense to his fucked up brain, but it didn't make sense to mine.

We were led across the hardwood floor and through a door at the back of the house. The only furniture in the room was a narrow bed and a couple of small chairs.

A row of restraints like those in the shed were attached to one wall. They took Ben to these and snapped the shackles around his wrists so he faced the room. A faint grimace was the only sign of his discomfort. He could either sit with his arms above his head, or crouch. There was no way for him to get truly comfortable.

That, I guessed, was the point.

"Get her over here," Dagen gestured towards the bed.

I shuddered and resisted, digging my bare feet into the floor. The henchholes dragged me over and pushed me down on my back. My ankles and wrists were snapped into restraints at the top and bottom of the narrow bed frame.

This wasn't fucking good.

The only thing I could do was pick up my head and look over towards Ben.

He looked furious. Either at Dagen or at himself. Knowing him, he was angry at both.

I gave him a forced half smile of reassurance, then lowered my head back down and looked up at the ceiling.

*Icy calm*, I remind myself. Whatever he has planned, I can get through this.

"Good. The doctor is here," Dagen said. He sounded more smug than ever.

*What the fuck?*

I picked my head back up and looked around. Sure enough, there was a man in what looked like a white surgical coat. He was pushing one of those trolleys they have in hospitals. The kind that contains surgical instruments.

The witch, what was her name? Irina was right behind him.

"What the hells?" I asked. Fuck not being provocative. What the hells screwy shit was Dagen doing?

The doctor moved around to the side of me and picked up a needle. He tapped the side of it with his finger, before he slid it into my arm. "It's okay," he said softly. "You won't feel a thing."

"What the fuck?" I demanded. "Dagen? What are you doing?"

Ben looked like he was ready to pull the restraints right out of the wall. His face was red. A vein throbbed in his forehead.

Dagen moved over to the other side of me. He brushed hair off my temple, then ran his knuckles down my cheek.

"I'm just being responsible," he said.

His words sent a shiver down my spine.

"What are you talking about?" I asked. I didn't think I fucking wanted to know. Panic started to rise again but this time I let it. It was a perfectly rational response to whatever the hells was going on.

"Oh, you know what they say." He leaned down to whisper in my ear. "Be sure to spay and neuter your pets."

Forget panic and chills. His words sent disbelief, then red-hot fear flooding through me.

I shook my head vigourously. "No. No you can't. Even you can't be that—" I couldn't think of a word that went beyond evil. Whatever it was, that was him.

Everything was a blur and I realised I was crying.

I turned my head to plead with the doctor. "You can't do this. *Please.*" I tried to fight against the restraints, but the needle must have contained anaesthetic. I could barely move, much less fight.

I even glanced at the witch. She was concentrating on something. Whatever it was, she wouldn't meet my eyes.

Of course not, she was as bad as they were.

My eyes got heavier. My whole body felt like jelly. All I could do was say, "Please," over and over until my voice got faint even to my own ears. I wasn't sure if I was speaking out loud anymore. It might have just been my brain unwilling to comprehend what was happening.

"There, that's better," Dagen said soothingly. "Maybe I should keep you like this. You're a lot more... Compliant."

I stared at him with wide eyes. If I could shoot daggers at him I would. Or sporks. Or anything.

"You can't do this," Ben growled. The anguish in his voice threatened to break another part of me.

Dagen chuckled. "Why? So you can get her pregnant? No. The Keelan line ends here. With her. There will be no next-generation hells bent on revenge. The cycle ends. Now. But don't worry," he added lightly. "You'll both be awake to see it."

I couldn't feel it, but I was vaguely aware of the doctor and a couple of Dagen's men taking off my clothes and putting them aside on a chair. All nicely folded. How fucking thoughtful of them. The doctor even put a sheet over me, up to my belly. And another over my breasts.

As if I gave a shit about modesty right now.

As if I didn't want to lose my shit when he pressed a scalpel to my abdomen.

As if tears didn't slide down my cheeks at the tugging sensation as he slid out parts of me and set them aside in a kidney dish.

As if I didn't weep softly when they took away my ability to have children.

In the back of my mind I admitted I would be a shit mother, and I never planned on having babies, but the choice should have been mine to make.

*Mine. No one else's.*

Instead, I was surrounded by the enemy, while the doctor, his face expressionless, violated me in the worst way I could ever have imagined.

Sick as fuck didn't even start to describe what this was. This was sicker than the very lowest of the seven hells. The hell reserved for the worst of the worst.

I squeezed my eyes shut and gave into the sense of nothingness the anaesthetic gave me. If I couldn't feel anything physically, then I would pretend I couldn't feel anything emotionally. I spent years mastering the art of not feeling anything. I had to shut it off when my parents died, so I could survive. When Helen Dagen tried to teach me I was worthless, I boxed up my feelings so I didn't give in to her. On the surface, it looked like I did. I was quiet, shy, even meek. I didn't put a toe out of line. I didn't give her an excuse to beat me. That didn't mean she didn't do it anyway, when she got angry at something or someone, but the excuse never came from me. I hated myself at the time, but I did what I had to do to survive. I would do that now. I would feel nothing. I would be a block of ice. A whole fucking iceberg.

"There," Dagen said finally. "All done. That wasn't so bad, was it?"

I didn't give him the satisfaction of opening my eyes, or even twitching. I gave him nothing. Nothing at all.

While the doctor dabbed at my abdomen, Dagen whispered in my ear, "This is your second lesson, but not the last. This is just the beginning. When I am done with you, you will be broken. You will beg to hand over everything you own to me. There will be no bloody uprising, not this time. Just a melted bitch who will be grateful I let her be on her knees in front of me. Everything you have, your properties, your money, your power, your influence and your body, will be mine. Do you understand, bitch?"

I opened my eyes and looked into his filthy, repulsive face. "Don't. Call. Me. Bitch," I said coldly. I would freeze all of the hells over myself before any of that happened.

"I can see you're in denial," he said lightly. "Would you really prefer to see every white wolf in the state lying dead?"

Well, no, I wouldn't fucking prefer that. But I was also not going to let him break me. I would get out of here and make him regret ever having taken a breath.

I turned my face away from him. There was nothing he had to say that I wanted to hear.

"Get to work," he ordered. He walked away to speak to the doctor, leaving me to my thoughts until the witch stepped closer. He said something about healing me and felt a tingle of magic on my abdomen.

Evidently I wasn't going to be allowed the long recovery period from the operation. Whatever. I didn't particularly want to be vulnerable for weeks anyway.

My wrists and ankles were removed from the restraints and the sheets slid off my body.

"Get up and get dressed," Dagen ordered.

One of his men brought my clothes over and put them on the bed beside me. He didn't even try to hide the fact he was staring at my breasts as I struggled to sit up. I curled my lip at him, but he moved away without even a hint of embarrassment.

Silently, I added him to the list of people who would regret their behaviour towards me. Him and all the other men who watched me hop off the bed and dress.

All of them but Ben. His eyes were on my face. They were full of concern and anger. He clearly wanted to rip off a few heads as much as I did. He was supposed to keep me safe, but they stole that away from him and left him to crouch helplessly against the wall.

I would definitely let him kill a few black wolves before we were done. As many as he liked. I suspected that number might be high. Good. They deserved it. Every last one of them.

They fucked with the wrong people. They chose the wrong side. I would fuck back so hard, they would beg to be killed.

I buttoned up my blouse and tried not to look over at the kidney dish which sat on top of the surgical trolley. Truthfully, I couldn't tell by looking, what the doctor took. Enough, I guessed. I wasn't going to ask. The specifics didn't matter, it wasn't like they could put it back in now anyway.

"That looks tasty, wouldn't you say?" Dagen said lightly.

"You're a twisted son of an omega aren't you?" I asked. That was pretty much the lowest thing a wolf could be.

The comment obviously pissed him off, but he laughed. "It's good to see the doctor didn't take your sense of humour. I look forward to breaking that, too."

I might be poking the hornet's nest, but I said, "You can take my freedom, but you can never take my sense of humour. Especially around a joke like you."

Thanks to the anaesthetic, I barely felt the slap across my face. I staggered a couple of steps back before I was caught by Ben, who had just been released from his restraints.

"You are a slower learner, than I gave you credit for," Dagen said derisively. "Fortunately, I like a challenge. The more they fight, the more fun they are to break. Take them back to their room."

I took a step towards the door.

"Wait." Dagen waved at two of his men. "Shift."

Without hesitation, they stripped off and shifted. Their black wolf form might have been impressive except for the whole being-a-pack-of-assholes thing.

Ben's hands tightened on my arms, but Dagen picked up the bowl and sniffed the contents. He turned to flash me a smile, then scooped out what was inside and tossed a bit to each of the wolves.

They snatched it up and swallowed it down without bothering to chew.

I turned and retched.

"I thought you would have thicker skin, Elodie," Dagen said.

I looked back and met his gaze unwaveringly. "My biggest regret in life to date is not having you killed when you were younger, Alistair," I said coldly. "That's not a mistake I'll make again."

He laughed. "How cute you pretend you have any power left. You can make all the threats you want, but you can't do anything to me. On the other hand..." He waved the bowl at me. "I can do whatever I want to you. Get some rest. You're going to need it." He turned away, only to turn back a moment later. "And practice breathing through your nose. You're going to need that too." He smiled like he got a participation trophy and strode out of the room.

"He is a motherfucking piece of shit," I growled. I started to take a step in the direction he'd gone, but I was so wobbly on my feet I almost fell. Ben caught me and swept me up into his arms. Under any other circumstances, I would have growled at him for picking me up like I was a helpless child. The only good reason for carrying me anywhere was to take me to bed and fuck my brains out. Otherwise, I could walk, even on wobbly legs.

Today though, I didn't think my legs would hold me, and better he carry me than one of asshole's motherfuckers. Still, I hated the feeling that I was this vulnerable.

I was Ivory, the big bad she wolf, but right now I felt like little more than a tepid puddle of water than an ice queen. I wasn't even the kind people slip on and break their necks. I was the kind they wiped up with a towel with barely a second thought.

"I've got her," Ben said firmly. "I'm not going to argue, or try anything. She needs to rest."

I hoped he *would* try anything if an opportunity arose, but that was going to be a lot harder when he was carrying me. But I was selfish and didn't insist he put me down. The warmth of his body and the anticipation of revenge were the only things keeping me going right now. I couldn't decide which one was more compelling than the other. They might be equal.

With what felt like no effort at all, Ben carried me up the stairs and back into the pretty cell where we'd spent the night.

Someone had left a fresh tray of food on the table, but I had no appetite. The smell of it made my stomach turn. At least I knew I wouldn't be eating anything from myself. Yeah, okay I recognised how sick that thought was. But I wouldn't have put it past Dagen to try that. I didn't think there was anything he wouldn't do to fuck with me.

The door closed and locked behind us and we were alone. For now.

Ben lowered me down to the bed and sat beside me. "I won't ask if you're okay. Not even you would be okay after that, and you are the most badass woman I've ever met."

"You need to get out more," I said dryly.

He laughed softly. "I'm working on it, believe me. Sooner or later he and his assholes are going to make a mistake. When they do, we'll be out of here." After a moment he added, "Of course, their first mistake was messing with you to begin with."

It sounded like he had more faith in me than I had in myself.

I couldn't help it. I started to cry. Just softly, and with tears that rolled down my cheeks so slowly they were cold before they dripped off my chin, but crying nonetheless.

Ben put his arms around me and drew me to him, so my face was pressed against his chest. He rubbed my back and whispered words I couldn't make out. The tone was soothing.

My body shook with silent sobs for a good five to ten minutes before I started to wear myself out. I lay against him for a good while longer.

"I wish you were somewhere away from here and safe," I said. "But, selfishly, I'm glad I'm not alone."

He kissed the top of my head. "I wish we were both somewhere else, but I'm glad I'm here for you. We will get out of here. I promise. Whatever it takes."

Whatever it takes. His words echoed through my mind. That was what worried me.

What might it take?

6

WE WERE LEFT ALONE for three days. Someone delivered food three times a day, always much more than we could eat.

I didn't have much of an appetite. I ate because I had to. And because Ben gave me long, worried looks if I didn't. I was pretty sure he was trying to channel Jake, except he didn't say a word when for dinner I ate a slice of cake left over from the lunch tray. It wasn't very good cake, and by the time I ate it, it was stale.

Whatever, it was sugar.

Ben and I took turns pacing across the room. Partly for exercise, and partly just to burn off our frustrations at being locked inside. I never thought I would wish for a treadmill, but after two days, I would have liked to run.

"I know this is all part of his plan, but it's pissing me off." I stomped across the room and back again. "I can be patient if I know what I'm waiting for. Although, whatever we're waiting for is bound to be shit."

"Probably," Ben agreed. He sat back on the couch, long legs crossed at the knees. Even when he was pacing, the man looked calm. Of course, it was his job to keep his cool at all times. Hells, it was my job too, but a thousand scenarios ran through my head while Dagen kept us waiting. Most of them involved my blood, his cock or both. Nothing I wanted to think about. So of course, it was all I could think about.

I focused on Jake and Cooper and what they were doing right now. I knew they were still alive, or Dagen would have come in here to brag. I also knew he hadn't found them, or he would have dragged Jake in front of me, or vice versa. While they were still out there, there was some hope. At least hope that my organisation would survive long after I did, out of the hands of Dagen and the Onyx Ridge pack.

I barely managed to contain a startle as the door swung open.

Dagen himself strode into the room, several of his asshole minions following on his tail.

"Are you enjoying the accommodation?" He gave me one of his best slimy-as-fuck smiles.

I responded with an eye roll and said, "Fuck off." Maybe I was poking the beehive again, but it was getting harder and harder to think what he might do that was worse than what he already did.

He raised one eyebrow at me. "That's why I'm here."

I forced myself to stand my ground, when I really wanted to take several steps back. Into last week. Maybe the week before. That would give me time to avoid this happening.

Ben rose and moved to stand behind me, his hands on my shoulders.

In some ways that made it easier, and in some it made it harder. His support meant the world to me, but he wasn't going to be able to stop Dagen from doing whatever he wanted.

Dagen put a hand in his pocket and pulled out a stone suspended on a leather cord.

My eyes widened involuntarily.

*Fuck.*

"I see you know what this is," Dagen said. "I have to admit, it wasn't easy to find a bonding stone with bonding magic in it. Even with money and resources, they are rare. But you know what it's like. If you want something badly enough, you can get it." He raised the stone up in front of his face and smiled at me past it.

"It's pretty, isn't it?"

I shrugged as if I didn't care. "It looks like a rock to me."

"Appearances can be deceiving." He stepped closer to me.

I swallowed and started to tremble. Ben's hands tightened on my shoulders.

"You have a choice to make," Dagen said slowly. "I'm going to put this around your neck. You know what that means." Before I could say anything," he added, "You'll form a bond with the next man who fucks you. Specifically, ejaculates into you."

I eyed the stone. "No shit. I choose to *not* have that happen."

He chuckled. "That isn't your choice. You get to choose to fuck your bodyguard."

Ben twitched.

I looked at him over my shoulder. "So you can beat the shit out of him and I could feel everything he's going through?" What the hells kind of choice was that?

"I can take it," Ben said firmly.

I half turned to face him. "And you would feel everything he does to me." Asking anyone to share my fucked up mind and emotions was a lot. Too much.

I turned back to Dagen. "What's the other choice?"

The smile he gave me sent a shiver down my spine. "I fuck you. You'll have all the fun of seeing yourself through my eyes. And I'll have the fun of feeling you break."

"She chooses me," Ben said. "Whatever you do to me will be better than you touching her."

Dagen smirked at him. Of course he knew what the choice would be. "Looks like the bodyguard's feelings go deeper than just a working relationship. Isn't that sweet? You have an hour. If a bond isn't formed by then, it's my turn." He slipped the cord around my neck and made sure the bonding stone touched my skin.

"It doesn't matter if you take it off now. It's touched you. The magic is under your skin, where it will stay for a couple of hours."

Ben's grip on my shoulders was almost painful. I thought he might change his mind once he remembered magic was involved. Was that another one of Dagen's tricks, or just an unlucky coincidence?

"Get to it then," Dagen said. He crossed his arms over his chest.

"What, no privacy?" Apparently there was too much to ask for.

"Pretend you're on the third floor at Crimson," Dagen said. "Performing in front of the crowds."

"Crimson is more tastefully decorated than this place," I said dryly. With a barely contained sigh, I turned to face Ben. He looked to be thinking.

"I'd like to make this as easy on you as possible," he said softly.

I appreciated the sentiment, but there were seven other men in the room. Nothing about this was going to be easy.

He leaned down to whisper in my ear. "For what it's worth, I want you. Very much." He caught my mouth in a tentative kiss that suggested he didn't mind being watched. Or preferred that to watching Dagen force himself on me again. Yeah, that was a no-brainer.

Truthfully, I didn't mind being watched. Even by Dagen, as fucked up as that was. Maybe we could teach him what sex looked like when two people cared about each other.

I let myself be caught up in the moment. It was just Ben and I. No one else was in the room with us. Our tongues danced. His hands slid up and down my sides. He led me over to the bed and lay me down before he lay over me, his body shielding mine from view.

He kissed my neck and around my throat. He kissed the top of my chest and I knew he wanted to lick and suck my nipples. Instead, he left my blouse and bra in place and kissed his way back up to my mouth. With one hand, he pulled my skirt up high enough to work his fingers underneath. His fingertips grazed the front of my panties.

My hands wandered down to caress his already half-erect cock through the fabric of his pants. I admit, I was impressed at his ability to be aroused when he had to be. I suspected Dagen assumed he wouldn't be able to perform. That would give him the excuse to step in. But, no, Ben was ready when I needed him. The man was a fucking hero.

Yeah, okay, part of me was terrified of what Dagen would use this bond for, but at least I could enjoy Ben's cock for a while. And very much appreciate the fact it wasn't Dagen's.

Ben tugged my panties down far enough for me to kick them off.

I unzipped his pants and pulled them down to free his erection. I was tempted to look at Dagen, to see if he was envious of the size of Ben's cock.

When Ben's hand slid across the seam of my pussy, I forgot all about Dagen again. All I could think about was having Ben inside me. I doubted an orgasm was in my immediate future, but I was wet enough for his cock.

I hitched my skirt up just enough to spread my knees and pull him into position.

His eyes firmly fixed on mine, Ben slowly slid into my body, bit by bit. Every couple of seconds, he would stop and let me adjust to his width, and make sure I was okay.

I was as okay as I could be, under the circumstances. His cock felt amazing and I wanted him to fuck me with it for hours. Anywhere but here.

I kept my eyes on his and gave him a tentative smile. "I'm all right," I said softly. "You feel amazing."

"You feel pretty incredible yourself," he said with a smile. "Is it wrong that I want to fuck you, no matter where we are?"

"When you're hot, you're hot," I said jokingly.

"You are definitely hot." He claimed my mouth again in a searing kiss. At the same time, his hips started to move, thrusting slowly, then with increasing speed.

In spite of my assumption, I got more and more aroused with every thrust into my slick core. I wanted him to tear off my clothes and taste every part of me. I wanted to do the same to him. I sent a little prayer to the gods that we could do that some-day. For now, this needed to be quick, not thorough.

His strokes became gradually faster and faster, in time with the pounding of my heart and the racing of my blood.

I slid my hands up the back of his shirt, my nails grazing the skin of his back.

"Fuck, that feels good," he whispered. "Nothing is better than the claws of my she wolf. Except her pussy." He thrust faster. His breathing became as ragged as mine.

My claws dug into his skin as I came. There was no screaming, no moaning, just a soft panting and a wash of pleasure that swept me away until it too was gone.

Ben came a moment later, with a series of quick, hard strokes. He gave out a soft, long, low groan and ground his hips against me. He thrust a few more times before exhaling out his nose and sagging down beside me.

A moment later I became aware of his feelings. Relief, pleasure and a deeper sense of love than I expected.

He picked up his head and we blinked at each other for a while before he smiled. "This is... Different."

I snorted. "Welcome to my fucked up feelings."

"Not fucked up," he said firmly, but gently. "Intense, but beautiful. Just like the outside you."

I didn't even see Dagen coming until two of his assholes grabbed Ben's arms and pulled him away from me. Another one drove his fist into Ben's stomach.

I gasped, unable to contain the surprise of not only the assault, but the way I felt Ben's pain through the bond. Fuck, that asshole could hit hard.

Dagen nodded, satisfied. "Okay, let him go." He gave me a smarmy smile. "I had to be sure."

I tugged my skirt down. "You could have just asked."

"Would you have told me the truth?" he asked.

"Considering the choice was to be fucked by you, then yes, I would have," I said coldly. "The bonding stone did its shit." I pulled the cord from around my neck and tossed the stone to the floor. I got to my feet and straightened my clothes. My heart was racing like crazy. I had, of course, considered the possibility that having Ben bond me was an experiment. Dagen wanted to know for sure that it was possible before he bonded me.

I waited for him to make a move towards me, but he didn't. Instead, he scooped up the bonding stone and put it back in his pocket.

"Enjoy your bond. We'll put it to a little test later." He gave me a smile before he swept out of the room, followed by his goons.

"Any guesses as to exactly how many screws he has loose?" I waited until the door was locked before I turned back to Ben.

He stood leaning forward, his hands on his stomach, a grimace on his face. When he saw me looking, he straightened up and schooled his expression back to calm.

I wasn't fooled for a moment, but I let him keep his dignity. He deserved that and more.

"My guess is at least twenty-seven," I said.

Ben smiled and sat back down on the couch. "My guess would be thirty-two. With at least another three or four missing."

"At least," I agreed. "Are you okay?" I sat down beside him.

He put an arm around me to draw me closer. "I'm

alone with the most beautiful woman in the world, with a bond to her no one else has, not even Jake. This should be pretty fucking perfect."

"That's a whole lot of irony for a Sunday," I said. I cocked my head. "It is Sunday, isn't it?"

Ben shrugged. "I have no idea. It feels like a Sunday."

"In that case, I dread to think what Monday might bring. You know whatever he has planned is going to be shitty. For some reason he didn't want to form a bond with me. Probably because I'm too amazing for him, and also I would know all his plans. Or have a better idea of them anyway. He said the magic wears off in a couple of hours, so he won't touch me until then. After that…"

"I hate magic," Ben said. "But if it keeps him away from you, then I hope it lasts for a long time. You know this bond will, don't you? As far as I know, it will last until one of us is dead."

"I would much rather be bonded to you for the rest of my life, than bonded to Dagen for even five minutes." The idea made my stomach twist. I didn't want him to touch me in the first place, but add a bond to that, it was pretty much worst nightmare material. Although, if there was anything I'd learnt from Dagen, it was that my idea of a worst nightmare wasn't as bad as anything he could think up.

"I would also prefer to be bonded to you than him," Ben said. "For a moment there I thought he was suggesting that. That he or one of his men…"

I looked at Ben in horror. "Gods, don't give him any ideas."The idea of being raped was bad enough. The thought of watching and feeling while someone raped Ben was enough to push my sanity down half a notch. I wasn't sure I could handle having that happen to someone I cared about. And I cared about Ben deeply. More and more as the days went on. It wasn't just the forced proximity, or his calming presence. I saw sides to him I hadn't known were there before. And I liked it. And for some reason, he liked me in spite of the fact everything he was going through was because of me.

"It's not on my wish list," he said. He kissed my forehead. "I can think of a few other things to wish for."

"Freedom," I said. "Bacon that's cooked properly. Some decent cheese. The jellybeans we never got to eat."

"A big, juicy hamburger," he added to the list. "The kind with beetroot on it."

I wrinkled my nose. "Really? Beetroot?"

He shrugged one shoulder. "I like the way it stains my fingers. It looks like blood."

"Oh." I nodded. "That makes sense." I glanced towards the door. "How long do you think it will be this time? They might keep us waiting for another three days. Or four. Or a week."

"Hmmm. What could we do to pass the time for a week?" He wiggled his brows at me. Before I could say anything, he said, "Hear me out. I'll know exactly what you like, because I'll be able to feel it. What better way to see how this bond works?"

Men.

"Yes, I'm sure that's exactly why some witch invented bonding magic," I said sarcastically. "So they could fuck better."

"I know several witches who would have invented it for exactly that," Ben said. "They wouldn't have invented it for romantic reasons."

"I suppose it is a good way to use magic," I conceded. More than that, I wouldn't have to explain why he needed to keep his cock away from my mouth. That was something I was *not* ready for.

Just the thought of it made me start to tremble again. In a matter of moments, I was back on the edge of panic.

"Oh gods," Ben said. "I'm sorry I didn't mean to—

fuck." He ran a hand over his head. "I shouldn't have—"

I shook my head. "It's not your fault." I leaned forward over my knees and tried to catch a breath. I tried to think about anything else, but the memory of his cock in my mouth crashed over me. I gagged like it was happening all over again.

I tried to suck in a breath, but it got caught in my throat and I squeaked instead.

Ben put his hands on my shoulders. "Breathe. Come on, my beautiful she wolf. Breathe. He's not here. It's just you and me. If I could take away your pain, I would do it. I would take all of it. Every drop. But you know what? We will not let him win. I'll kill him with my bare hands if that's the last thing I do. It will be worth it."

I managed to regain enough of my composure to say, "He deserves to die painfully and slowly. I don't know how, but I'm going to make that happen." I was sure of that as I was sure I was still Ivory, the big bad she wolf. He would pay dearly for everything he did.

7

It was four days, in the end. After I got over my panic attack, and had a very ordinary cheese sandwich for lunch, I took Ben back to bed to test his theory. As it turns out, he was right. The moment he discovered how much I like having my nipples sucked, he spent a good hour or two doing just that. With no one to watch us, and really nothing else to do, we spent a lot of time exploring each other's bodies and getting closer.

The whole time, I couldn't help but think our time together was coming to an end. I didn't know how or why, but I savoured every moment as if it was the last.

We were sitting on the couch talking about

nothing in particular when the door finally opened again.

"Let's play a game," Dagen said as he stepped into the room.

I cocked my head at him, then looked around him. "I don't see anyone with a Monopoly board." Thank the gods for that, I hated Monopoly. Still, there were worse games to play. I had a feeling we were about to find that out.

Dagen laughed. "I've already won the Monopoly. Or I will, very soon."

"Really? I would have thought you're the kind of man who would tip the board over when you're losing." I rose to my feet.

"I might," he actually agreed. "But I'm winning. Take them downstairs to the lawn."

There was something about the words that sent a chill down my spine. I glanced over to Ben who sent thoughts of reassurance. At least one of us was confident.

We were taken back down to the grass near the shed.

Four more of his henchholes waited there for us.

And Hutton.

Judging by the bruises and blood on Hutton's sullen face, and the way two goons held his arms,

Dagen decided he wasn't on his side. I guessed that meant he was on mine. The timing sucked, but the relief was real. In spite of Jake's misgivings, I liked the guy.

Hutton glanced at me like he didn't recognise me. His shoulder twitched like a tiny shrug. He must have been caught doing something he shouldn't have. That was the only sign I got that he knew I existed.

I returned his glance with one of indifference.

"Did you think I'd be fooled?" Dagen asked. "By a white wolf amongst my men?"

I turned my indifference on him. "He's a traitor to our kind. He might as well be a black wolf. Those guys Gus corrupted are beyond saving." Some didn't take it well when I took back my territory. They got used to being able to kill indiscriminately. One or two died defending black wolves. A few more were disposed of quietly. No one took pleasure in that. It wasn't too surprising Jake didn't trust Hutton. The past was murky at best.

"Then you won't miss him when he's dead," Dagen said lightly.

I matched his tone. "I guess not."

To Hutton's credit, his expression didn't change. I had no idea if he was pissed off, or understood I was pretending I didn't care for his sake. I got nothing from him at all. A total closed book. He could have taken lessons in being carved ice from me.

"As for your bodyguard," Dagen went on, "you're going to miss him a little bit more. Or his cock anyway. Don't worry, mine will console you. Now you can't get pregnant, you'll be a lot more fun."

Yeah, I figured that was the point of the surgery. Not just that I couldn't breed, but that he couldn't breed with me. That was a small blessing, I supposed. Carrying his whelp would be a whole other nightmare.

"No thank you," I said, my voice frozen steel. I somehow managed to keep myself from trembling. I forced the flashbacks into the rear of my brain. "I don't want your cock, and I don't want to play games. This bullshit has gone on long enough. You think you're going to break me, but you won't." He'd have to kill me first.

Dagen leaned in closer. "That's what they all say. Right before they break." He reached up and pinched my nipple through the fabric of my bra. Just when I thought he might let it go, he twisted it so hard I let out a tiny gasp of pain. "I've barely started."

In the corner of my eye, I saw Ben take a step towards us before a couple of Dagen's men grabbed him. I felt his anger. How much he wanted to rip Dagen to pieces.

I shook my head. He should be looking for a chance to get out of here. Get away. Run.

He sent back thoughts; he didn't want to leave without me.

*If you get a chance, you have to go, that's an order.* I couldn't tell him in words, but those were the feelings I sent to him. He wanted to resist, I felt that through the bond too, but I was firm.

Dagen let go of my nipple and pushed me away. "I know you want me, but you'll have to wait. Our game comes first."

I staggered back but managed to stay on my feet. It was getting harder and harder to keep my composure. More difficult still when some of Dagen's men started to undress. For a moment, I thought I was the toy in this game.

Then they shifted and cold dread formed in my stomach.

"I see you understand," Dagen said smoothly. "It's been a while since we've had a good old-fashioned hunt. I've been looking forward to it. It's entertaining and a good way to get rid of two white wolves. The rules are simple. Hutton and the bodyguard will get a minute head start. In fact, I'm feeling generous. Make it two minutes. Then the black wolves will give chase. Whoever catches and kills them, wins. In fact," he smiled as though he was a game show host or something, "whoever kills them, can fuck the bitch after I do. With her lovers' blood all over them."

I wanted to call him a sick fuck, but it was something I probably would have thought up myself. Blood and fucking are a perfect combination. Blood and rape, however, were a different story.

Two henchholes held Ben, while the witch crossed the lawn and removed his collar with a snap.

I both saw and felt what he was thinking.

He could shift and go after Dagen.

*You have your orders. Shift and get the fuck out of here.* My expression was firm. If he stuck around, they would kill him. I was certain of that. This might be his only chance. He *had* to take it. Even if I never saw him again, I needed him to be safe. If he died, if either of them did…I might break after all.

Ben's expression was defiant. He hesitated, but I was insistent. He nodded reluctantly, then glanced at Hutton. Something passed between them. Something silent, but almost palpable.

I didn't know what it meant, but the two men had come to some kind of understanding.

Dagen glanced at his watch. "Your two minutes starts… Now."

Ben and Hutton shifted simultaneously, shredding their clothes in the process. They bounded off towards the trees, headed in opposite directions. Two white, magnificent wolves.

Barely two minutes later, Dagen nodded towards his wolves. With barely a sound, they started off after Hutton and Ben. Half one way, half the other.

I thought about making a run for it, but several goons remained arrayed around me. Far enough to give me some space, but close enough to react if I moved. Dagen was excited enough without me provoking him further.

Another man leaned against the side of the shed, a cigarette hanging from the corner of his lips. Not a goon, if his outfit was anything to go by.

He pushed himself off the wall and walked toward me.

"How about we sneak off and get to the end bit of this?" he suggested. He gave me a wink to show he was joking. For some reason, I sensed he was harmless. No, harmless wasn't the word. Just… less likely to rape me. That didn't mean I lowered my guard. Not for a second.

"What would the boss think?" I nodded towards

Dagen. He was watching the trees intently, obviously enjoying the idea of his men killing Ben and Hutton.

The guy shrugged one shoulder and ashed his cigarette on the grass. "He doesn't pull my strings. He just pays me to do a job once in a while."

I looked more closely. He wore a long, black leather jacket. His neat beard held a sprinkle of grey. His dark hair was pulled back, the top tied in a ponytail. I guessed he was around the same age as Jake.

"Lucifer Fisher," I said.

He gave me a half bow. "In the flesh. And you're Ivory."

I didn't need to confirm that he was right. Who else would I be? "What is an assassin doing here?" I presumed he hadn't come to kill me. Or take part in the hunt.

"Would you believe I came to the area to surf?" he asked.

"No," I said simply. My attention was half on the conversation and half on feeling Ben run. The bush was thick, and it was slow going. What slowed him down also slowed down his pursuers. I tried not to let my fear for him bleed out into the bond. Now would be a really bad time for him to be distracted.

"They said you were smart," the assassin said approvingly.

I cocked my head at him. "They said you were stealthy. But here you are, standing right in front of me."

"If I didn't want you to see me, you wouldn't," he said. "Being an assassin is a lonely job. Sometimes I like to have a conversation with someone who's not…" He nodded towards Dagen.

"An asshole psychopath?" I guessed.

He chuckled softly. "Something like that. Some of us aren't happy the Onyx Ridge pack's name is being sullied by an alpha who doesn't have all of our best interests at heart."

That surprised me. Not that he was thinking it, but that he would come out and say it with Dagen standing a few metres away. Not to mention his goons who were even closer.

"Those are brave words, Lucifer Fisher," I told him.

"Call me Luca," he said. "I'm not scared of Alistair Dagen. I'm much more scared of you." He gave me a lopsided smile and pulled out another cigarette. He offered me one before lighting his.

I shook my head to decline the offer. "Under most circumstances, I would suggest it's wise to be scared of me," I said. Anyone with any sense should be. I had a long memory and a lot of resources. "I seem to be slightly disadvantaged right now."

"A situation I'm sure you will remedy before too much longer," he assured me. He took a long draw on his cigarette. "Alistair's dislike of women means he tends to underestimate them."

This assassin seemed to have more faith in me than I had in myself. It was strangely gratifying.

"I'm starting to think you know something I don't," I said. "If the black wolves are planning a coup, you have my full support."

Luca looked amused at that. "If we were planning anything, would I tell you? At the end of the day, you're still the enemy."

I thought about that for a moment. "Sometimes we end up in bed with people we don't expect to end up in bed with. For mutual benefit."

He nodded and dropped his cigarette butt to the grass. He put it out with his heel. "So if any of us were planning anything, you would help if it was to your benefit?"

"I might be persuaded," I agreed. "Whoever replaced the current asshole would have to be an improvement. Would it be you?"

Now he looked surprised. "Me? Gods no." He

laughed. "No black wolf in their right mind would follow me."

"Why not?" I asked. "They follow him. Surely he is the bottom of the barrel, not the top."

Luca shrugged and pulled out another cigarette. "He has a lot of support because of who his parents were." He looked at me like he was suggesting that was the reason people supported me.

"Sometimes parentage is a good reason *not* to follow someone," I said dryly. "No one could claim my parents were saints. My father had more mistresses than he had hair on his head. My mother was… Let's just say she wouldn't have won mother of the year." She was distant at best.

"And you've risen above all of that," Luca said.

Let's see, I had a few boyfriends, if you wanted to call them that. If I was still able to have children, I would be distant like my mother, busy, distracted. Maybe I was more like my parents than I'd like to admit.

I pushed down the panic that threatened to rise at the memory of the surgery. I couldn't let that leak into the bond with Ben either.

He had run through a small stream and was currently lurking in some bushes near the fence line.

"I can't claim to be perfect," I said slowly. "But I

wouldn't do the things Dagen does. Even if I had the equipment. If I had to choose between me and him, I would align with me."

"And how would the rest of the white wolves feel about working with black wolves?" Luca asked. "That is an old hate that runs deep."

"That's true," I admitted. "It wouldn't be easy." For all my talk about supporting a coup, it would be very difficult for me to put my own prejudice aside and work with them. It might be impossible for Jake. For Ben too. For him it would be like working with witches. Cooper was the only one too young to have lived through what the rest of us did. Lucky him.

"So," I said slowly. "Is there a plan?"

"Not that I know of," Luca said. "But like I said, if there was, I wouldn't tell you. No offence."

"None taken," I said. "Just think about what I said."

He pulled a lighter out of his pocket and lit his third cigarette. "How is your boy doing?"

It took me a moment to realise he knew about the bond. How? I was tempted to ask, but no doubt Dagen's goons liked to gossip.

"He's still alive," I said. He was no closer to finding a way out through the fence though. I hoped to the gods there was one. Obviously the point of this hunt, and the bond, was to have me feel the moment Dagen's men ripped Ben to pieces. It would be like killing me, but I would still be alive. If he wanted me to break, that would certainly expedite the process. It was a simple, but fucked up plan. Just the way Dagen liked it.

"Why aren't you taking part?" I asked. "I thought an assassin would enjoy killing."

Luca raised his eyebrows at me. "I prefer subtler methods. And I like a challenge. A handful of black wolves against two white ones... The odds aren't really in their favour."

That was true. If Ben couldn't find a way out through the fence, then he didn't stand much of a chance against his pursuers.

Same with Hutton, wherever he was. The baying of wolves sounded distant. He could have led them a long way from the house. What had passed between him and Ben? A plan to separate? To give themselves half a chance? Maybe they hoped to draw all of the black wolves after one of them, giving the other guy a free pass.

Who knows what men are thinking on any given day?

"Even if you got to fuck me afterwards?" I asked bluntly.

"Considering Alistair wasn't factoring consent into his gracious offer," Luca said ironically, "I'm not interested." He gave me a slow smile. "Do I look like the kind of guy who needs to force himself on a woman?"

I couldn't help but smile back. "You look like the kind of guy who would charm the pants off even a white wolf. Under different circumstances, of course."

He inclined his head. "Of course. You're not what I expected."

I snorted. "Neither are you. You're very articulate for a black wolf."

"And for a white wolf, you don't have your head up your ass," he said. "And you haven't threatened me yet."

"Would you like me to?" I asked sweetly. "I'm sure I could think of something."

He chuckled. "I'm sure you could. So could I. You are, after all, still surrounded by black wolves."

I sighed. "Don't remind me." They were closing in on Ben. I could feel his heart pounding. My sense that we were running out of time was stronger now. A sliver of fear crept up my spine. My gaze turned towards Dagen. He looked excited, like he knew the end was close. It was only a matter of time before he turned that excitement on me.

"Has anyone ever asked you to assassinate themselves?" I asked.

"Are you asking me to?" Luca asked. I couldn't tell what he thought of the suggestion.

I shrugged. "You know what's going to happen to me."

"I also know death is very permanent," he said. "Don't go asking for it until you're sure. And you have a way to be sure I get paid for it. After all, Alistair would be pissed off if I did it. It would have to be worth it."

"Sorry, I seem to be without my phone," I said. "Maybe I could borrow yours?" It was worth a try, right?

Before he could answer, the bush in front of us burst into flames.

8

---

ALL HELLS BROKE LOOSE. The baying of wolves turned to screams of pain and fear. The air was thick with it. That and smoke.

Through the bond I felt Ben's surprise, a flash of terror, then relief. He darted through a hole in the fence that hadn't been there a moment ago. It was hot. So hot he was worried it would catch his fur on fire. Then he was through and bounding out the other side.

The black wolves followed him through, right on his tail. But then they froze.

He was surrounded. By people and white wolves. Familiar faces. Hutton. Cooper.

*Jake.*

I wanted to sob, but I clung to my composure.

"Fuck," Dagen swore. His face was red with fury. He rounded on me. "What did you do, *bitch?*" Of course, he had no way to know what was going on beyond the fire that was quickly spreading through the trees. Unless he had a bond with one of the hunters. If so, I hoped he had an agonising, slow death. Just like the one Dagen deserved.

"What?" I asked innocently. "I've been standing here the whole time." I backed up a step, and hated myself for doing it, but his expression was pure murder. More than that, he looked like he was ready to tear me apart with his bare hands. And take his time doing it.

He saw my reaction and smiled.

*Smiled.*

He was a fucking bully who got off on scaring people who were less able to fight back.

"Get the bitch around to the back of the house. We need to evacuate." At least he had that much sense.

A tree about fifty metres away exploded. A heavy branch was thrown so far it smashed into the bath-house. Everything inside that was flammable immediately caught fire.

That was the distraction I needed. I cursed the fucking collar that prevented me from shifting, and bolted as fast as I could across the grass and away from the house. I headed towards the driveway and hoped like hells it was wide enough to act as a firebreak.

Behind me, Dagen shouted. I glanced over my shoulder as a couple of goons started after me, but the rest followed Dagen towards the back of the house.

Coward.

He probably thought the fire would take care of me so he didn't have to. Or he was just thinking about saving his own ass, and that his men would deal with me.

The further I ran, the thicker the smoke became. It got into my lungs, made it harder and harder to breathe.

A sensible person would probably turn and run the other way. I could let Dagen's men grab me and get the hells away from the growing flames. I weighed up my options and decided that I would prefer to face the fire than the things Alistair Dagen would do to me. Maybe that made me a coward. Maybe it didn't.

These last couple of weeks had proved there were worse things than dying.

The smoke made my eyes water. I coughed and blinked away tears. The only consolation was that my pursuers were suffering as much as I was.

Through the bond, Ben sent thoughts of reassurance. He was close.

The men behind me were closer. Their shoes pounded on the gravel. They must be so sure they could catch me, they didn't even bother to shift. They might be right.

I threw out my hands to protect my face as a tree exploded a couple of metres away. Heat washed over me like a furnace. It was moments like this when I remembered I wasn't made of actual ice. I would melt the same as anyone else.

I sensed Ben's worry. He wanted to come to me. He was telling Jake and Cooper where I was. They were getting frantic.

I sent back thoughts that I was fine. They needed to stay where they were. That was an order. I added my relief that Ben was safe. If I didn't get out of this, at least he had. Hutton too.

Another tree exploded. I narrowly avoided being hit by a red-hot branch. I swerved at the last moment but slowed enough for one of Dagen's men to grab my arm.

"Are you crazy?" he hissed. "We need to get the fuck out of here."

"Go ahead," I said between coughs. "Tell your boss I'm dead." I would be if we stood here for much longer. So would the guy whose fingers dug into my skin.

"Come on." He tried to drag me back towards the house. His companion caught up with us and grabbed me by my other arm.

We were all coughing now.

"You two can get out of here alive if you shift," I pointed out. "I can't shift, all I'll do is slow you down."

I was right and they knew it. I saw it on their faces. "I can't run any faster. You saw me." I turned my face and wiped tears on my sleeve. "Save your own asses. Dying in a fucking fire is above your pay grade."

They exchanged glances. They might also kill me, then run, but that would waste valuable seconds. Both knew that too.

One nodded. "I hope you die painfully, bitch." He shifted and loped back towards the house. His companion followed half a second later.

"Right back at you," I told them. I waited for a tree to explode and take them out, but instead they safely disappeared from view.

Shame. I was getting really, really tired of being called bitch.

I staggered back down the driveway, but my thoughts were foggy. Smoke inhalation, I knew, was worse than the flames themselves.

The smoke was so thick now it was getting more and more difficult to tell the difference between driveway and brush. It was also getting harder to fight the urge to sit down. I could just give up, let the smoke take me, but fuck that. This was nowhere near the hardest thing I had ever done. I wasn't going to let it beat me. Not with the guys so bloody close.

"Ivory?" Jake's voice was the single sweetest sound I've ever heard, even though it was laced with fear.

I tried to shout back, but got caught up in a coughing fit.

"Ivory?" That was Cooper. "Where are you?"

Ben asked the same question, but through the bond. Gods, he felt so close.

My head was swimming now and my lungs were burning. I wanted to rip off the collar, shift and run the last—it couldn't be more than a handful of metres.

All I could do was let the tears stream down my cheeks and run blindly towards their voices, to where the bond took me.

I staggered past burning bushes and the twisted remains of the front gate. That was the surest sign I had that Jake had done exactly as I'd asked. I only knew of one person powerful enough to do that, and set the bush on fire.

"Ivory!" Jake shouted again. "She's over here."

I took a handful more steps before I fell into a strong, tattooed pair of arms.

"She needs a healer. Where is that witch? Paxton?" Jake shouted loud enough to make me wince. "Oh gods, sorry." He wiped the tears of my cheeks with his thumbs. "Elodie, I was so fucking—" He shook his head. "I thought..."

I spoke although my voice was hoarse and my throat burned like hells. "I'm okay." That was a flat out lie and we both knew it. "I will be."

"Ivory!" Cooper bounded towards me like a puppy. He threw his arms around me and gave me a squeeze. "Ben said you were okay, but I needed to see you. How did he know?"

I squeezed him back. "That's an answer for later."

I felt Ben before I saw him, and reached to lace my fingers into his.

We shared a look. The kind people share when they've been through something together only they would understand.

"I'm glad you're okay," he said softly.

"You too," I said.

Jake and Cooper looked surprised at this new intimacy between us, but neither seemed like they would question it. They were just relieved to see me and Ben alive.

Truthfully, I was pretty fucking relieved myself.

"You should sit down," Jake gestured towards one of the waiting cars.

Hutton sat on the ground, his back leaning against a tyre, face pale. Judging by the amount of blood on his skin, the black wolves caught up to him. A man with dark hair and a blonde-headed woman crouched beside him.

"Hutton told us where you were," Jake said. "Gave us a bunch of useful information, before he was caught. If it wasn't for Harmony and Paxton, he wouldn't have made it."

On hearing their names, the pair turned and rose. Ben stiffened.

Harmony was half witch, half demon. Presumably that was close enough to being a full witch for Ben's taste. Paxton Evans was a full witch, but if he saved Hutton, then he got a pass as far as I was concerned.

"She's breathed in a shit load of smoke," Jake said. He helped me to sit down beside Hutton.

"And I want this fucking collar off from around my neck," I said. I was tired of feeling like a pet dog.

"That should be easy enough," Paxton said. Judging by the look on his face, he clearly knew smoke and a magic collar weren't the only things wrong with me right now. They were the only things he could heal though.

He put a hand lightly on my arm. I felt the tingle of magic. Almost immediately, the burning in my lungs started to recede. With his other hand, he gripped the collar and it fell away from my neck. He glanced at it for a moment before handing it to Jake.

I nodded towards Harmony. She was pregnant when we first met and she was pregnant again now. I couldn't contain a pang of jealousy. It was going to take time to come to terms with what Dagen stole from me. I may never accept it, but I could try to be happy for her.

"I assume you started the fire?" I asked.

She smiled. "It wasn't exactly my intention. I was

trying to blast the gate open. Sometimes my magic does what I want it to. Sometimes not." She sighed through her nose and lightly rested a hand on her belly. "This little one was trying to help too. She doesn't understand restraint yet."

"Like her mother," Paxton said teasingly.

Harmony gave him a fond look, which he returned. She looked a lot more content when I saw her last.

"I appreciate it either way," I said. "This makes us even." She came to me a year or so ago, wanting a siphon stone so she could get back the magic which was stolen from her. I managed to secure a stone, but gave it to her with the condition that she owed me a favour. I had no idea at the time what that favour would be, but I thanked past me for the insight. Having Jake call on her to fulfil her end of the bargain saved my ass today. And Ben's and Hutton's too.

Having powerful people owe you a favour was worth more than money. I would have to see if I could find a way to do something else for her. It wouldn't hurt to have her in my pocket again. Just in case.

I heard the thrum of a helicopter engine. For a minute or two, I forgot all about Dagen. Now, I watched his chopper rise above the burning treetops and head off in a southerly direction.

"I knew I should have bought the helicopter and equipped it with missiles," Jake said darkly.

"Fuck," I said softly. "I don't suppose you brought a dragon with you?"

"I would have, but no one asked," Paxton said. "There, that will stop you from dying of smoke inhalation. It's going to take longer to fix the internal damage. I presume you'd rather not do that here." Shit, he was blunt.

Everyone's eyes were on me. Jake looked like he was ready to climb the tree tops and bring down the chopper himself.

*"Internal damage?"* he asked.

"It's nothing that can be fixed," I said softly.

"I can't put anything back," Paxton agreed. "But whoever healed you didn't heal everything. There's scar tissue that's going to be a problem if it's not dealt with." He muttered something about unskilled witches.

"What are you talking about?" Jake asked. "Put things back? What the fuck?"

"Later," Paxton snapped. "In case you hadn't noticed, the fire is spreading. Unless you want to get burnt to a crisp, I suggest we get out of here."

Jake quickly nodded. "Everyone, get into the cars." He reached for my hand. He and Ben helped me to my feet. From there, it was a step or two into the back seat of the closest vehicle. Jake headed around to the driver's side door, and Ben slid in next to me. To my surprise, Harmony and Paxton helped Hutton into the other side before they hurried to another car.

"Hey," I said softly to Hutton. "Seems like we have you to thank for getting out just in time."

He shrugged. "I did what you sent me in there to do. I found enough information on Dagen to even shut Jake up."

"Don't count on it," Jake said. He waited until Cooper slipped into the passenger seat before he gunned the engine and followed the other cars out towards the highway. "But you led us to Ivory, and for that I will be eternally grateful."

"But you still don't trust me?" Hutton said.

"That depends what information you found," Jake said. "Let's just say the jury is still out."

Hutton grunted under his breath.

"Jake will come around," Cooper said confidently. "You did almost get eaten by wolves."

I should probably step in and say something, or tell them to shut up, but all I wanted to do right now was lean against Ben, close my eyes and pretend the last couple of weeks never happened. Paxton's blunt tone, although clearly not intended to be hurtful, cut me right down to the bone. Somehow it made everything seem so much more painfully real.

"I know it doesn't seem like it right now, but you're going to be okay," Ben whispered in my ear. "You're the strongest person I know."

"I'm not sure about that," I said. "If it wasn't for you being there with me, I probably would have unravelled."

"No you wouldn't," he said. "You're Ivory. You wouldn't have let Dagen win. You still won't. If I was him, I would be shaking in my shoes."

"There is no way you would ever be him," I said firmly.

He put an arm around me and pulled me to his chest.

Cooper twisted around in his seat. "So, are you two a thing too?"

Jake turned his head just enough to hear without taking his eyes off the road.

I glanced over my shoulder at Ben. "We'll see." Honestly, right now I could barely think straight, much less make any kind of promises. There was still the chance the closeness was only because of what we endured. Once we got back to our lives, we might go back to boss and bodyguard. That might be all Ben wanted.

All of this was a conversation for later.

"You and I could be a thing if you give me a chance." Hutton gave me a cheeky grin.

"Like I said, we'll see," I said. "Can a girl rest for a while first?"

"Of course, take all the time you need," he replied easily. "Just don't take too long."

I managed a weary smile, but that was the best I could do right now.

Apparently not quite ready to let the matter lie, Jake said, "I don't know about the Hutton thing, but I trust Ben almost as much as I trust myself. Now I think about it, I'm not sure what took you two so long. I'm pretty sure Ben has been hot for you since he met you."

Ben chuckled. "He's not wrong." He didn't elaborate. Evidently he was willing to let the matter lie for a while. Or physical attraction was as far as it went, and this was his way of pulling back.

I looked out the window in silence and wondered what would have happened if I'd gone with Dagen. Could I somehow have stopped him from getting on that helicopter? Or better yet, thrown him off it? Or would he be taking all of his frustration out on me right now? It was probably just as well I would never know the answer to that. He would never have the opportunity again. If Jake had to handcuff me to him, he would never let me out of his sight again. That would chafe eventually, but I didn't want him out of my sight either. Any of the guys.

I cracked my eyes open. "What happened to Toby?" I asked Hutton.

"They were about to kill him when a guy in a leather jacket said he would deal with him," Hutton said. "He said he was part of the Onyx Ridge pack. Dagen's men seemed to know who he was. They handed him over."

I nodded. Luca Fisher, I presumed. That might mean there was hope for Toby yet. Or Luca had some agenda of his own. I had no doubt he did. Everyone had an agenda.

We reached the highway and headed south, a convoy of SUVs and other vehicles. Wolf shifters with black wolf blood on them, or their own blood. People like me, slightly charred and tainted with ash. But alive. The scratches and scrapes, bruises and dirt were nothing.

It was the internal shit that weighed heavily on my mind. I felt as though at some point, I was going to lose my shit completely. Unravel. Cry for a week or two. I didn't know when or where, I just knew it would happen.

I needed to hold it together as best I could in the meantime.

And make a plan.

Alistair Dagen would pay dearly for what he did to me.

9

"WHAT IS THIS PLACE?" We pulled up behind Paxton's white SUV outside a building on a quiet suburban street.

"It's a house that belongs to a friend of a friend," Jake said. "I figured the three of you would appreciate a chance to clean up before we got back to the city."

Considering I was a mess and Ben and Hutton were wrapped in old blankets found in the back of the car, that was a fair guess. There was more than likely more to it than that though. Regrouping. Debriefing. A thorough health check.

"That's very thoughtful," Hutton said with a hint of sarcasm.

Jake looked at his reflection in the rearview mirror. "Unless you want to walk the rest of the way…"

"If you don't stop, you can *both* walk the rest of the way," I growled. I was getting tired of their bickering. It was helpful to exactly no one and it made my frayed nerves worse.

Both guys actually shut up, but they still shot daggers at each other with their eyes.

Ben gave me a squeeze and helped me out of the car, even though I tried to wave off his help. Cooper was at my other elbow a moment later.

"If you guys are going to start to smother me…" I didn't know what I would do. I appreciated that they cared about me and wanted to look after me, but at this rate I would have to turn in my badass she wolf card and slink away with my tail between my legs. In spite of the last couple of weeks, I still wanted to believe I could take care of myself. I *could* take care of myself. I had done it since I was eight years old.

"We don't want to smother you," Cooper said. "We just love you. We were scared we would lose you. Well, I was. Jake said you would be okay. He said you wouldn't let a little thing like a kidnapping take you from us."

"That sounds like Jake." I gave Jake a look. I knew him better than that. He would have been just as worried as Cooper, if not more. He knew the shit Dagen was capable of. No doubt he was just trying to reassure Cooper.

"Did he let you kill anyone?" I asked.

Cooper sighed. "No. Not even Dagen's men. He left that to the other guys."

I patted his shoulder. "I'm sure there will be plenty of time for that later. There's lots of black wolves left in need of killing."

He brightened up. "Yeah, there are. I hope I can get in on it this time."

I exchanged glances with Ben. He looked amused, like he was listening to his kid brother talk about a playdate. I guessed he was, in a way. It did seem to be Cooper's idea of fun.

We walked up the front steps and entered the house after Jake unlocked the door.

"Nice place," Hutton said. "Cosy."

The whole house was smaller than the apartment at Crimson, but it would do.

"There's clothes in the wardrobe that should fit you all," Jake said. He waved vaguely towards one of the rooms.

"I'd like a word with Ivory," Paxton said. "In

private." After a moment he added, "Harmony can be in attendance if you're worried I can't keep my hands to myself." He looked like he was on the verge of an eye roll. He was a doctor after all. Hopefully a better one than the asshole who worked for Dagen.

"I'm sure there's nothing you could talk to her about that we can't hear," Jake said.

"Doctor/patient confidentiality," Paxton said. "You four are not impartial." He waved me towards another room like he wouldn't take no for an answer.

All four of the guys looked like they were ready to punch the shit out of him.

It was Harmony who put up her hands to defuse the situation. "Paxton wouldn't ask if it wasn't important. I'll keep a close eye on him."

Jake seemed unsure as to if he should trust either of them, but they had helped get me away from Dagen. That gave them a metric shit ton of credibility as far as I was concerned.

I nodded at the guys to back down.

"I'll be fine," I said. "I can take care of myself." Frankly, it wouldn't hurt to be checked over by an actual doctor, not that butcher Dagen hired, or the witch, Irina.

We headed into the other room and Harmony

closed the door softly behind us.

"I'll make this brief," Paxton said. "You were held prisoner by an asshole. That is not something you get over straightaway. You can ask Harmony. She knows all about it."

"Paxton kept me locked in a room for five months," she said lightly. "It really does fuck with your head. Well, it was Zeta, but he worked for them. Or *with* them. It's complicated."

Paxton shrugged. "I was trying to keep her safe."

I looked at them both in surprise. "If a man did that to me, I would cut off his balls."

Paxton responded to that with a wry smile. "What makes you think I have any balls left?"

I wasn't sure if he was joking or not, but Harmony grinned.

"So that's not yours then," I stated and waved at Harmony's belly.

She pressed her hands to her bump. "She's Jordan's. He's the guy who was with me when I asked for the siphon stone. He wanted to be here, but he is looking after our other baby. We're still in hiding from Zeta."

I nodded. "I appreciate you taking the chance to help me." Not that they had a choice.

"Yeah." Paxton nodded. "I wanted to finish the

healing I started up north. And give you a chance to talk about what happened with someone who is not going to get emotional and start beating their chest."

I wanted to deny that the guys would do that, but he was right. If I wanted to talk about things, it would be better to do that with someone impartial.

He put a hand on my arm. I felt the tingle of magic again. "He broke a cheekbone? The witch didn't heal it properly either."

"Dagen told her to leave the bruises." I stood still, trying not to show how disconcerting his touch was.

"She left more than that."

I felt movement under the skin, then Paxton nodded.

"That's better. Leg too? Anywhere else? Apart from your abdomen? You know you'll never have children?"

I nodded and tried to ignore Harmony's look of sympathy. She was much sweeter than I was.

Before I could respond verbally, Paxton added, "Vaginal tearing?"

I winced at how blunt the question was.

Even Harmony looked surprised.

"No," I said. "He didn't touch me there. Not my ass either," I added before he could ask.

"Is there any chance he drugged you and did

things you can't remember?" he asked. He lowered his hands and crossed his arms over his chest. "I know these questions are invasive, but they're important. You don't have to tell me, but tell someone. Get therapy. Whatever."

"Is that what you did?" I asked Harmony. I saw the fond looks she gave Paxton and wondered how the hells she ever forgave him. I mean, there's room in the world for all sorts of relationships, but if someone like Jake locked me up, I couldn't imagine forgiving him. I would probably let Cooper kill him. On the other hand, Jake would never do that.

I sighed. "No, I don't think he drugged me and did anything. Not unless he drugged Ben as well. It's not really his style though. He's a bully. He likes people to know what he's done. He likes an audience."

"Paxton," Harmony said softly. "Can you wait outside with the others?"

He hesitated for a moment, then nodded. "Take your time." He backed out the door and closed it behind him.

"I don't know about you, but I need to sit." Harmony lowered herself down to the bed in the middle of the room.

I took the hint and sat beside her. "Why don't you hate him?"

She glanced towards the door. "Paxton and I are complicated. Fucked up, absolutely. But we work. He understands me and I understand him. And yes, I have a very nice psychologist who helps me work through all this. And three other guys who help keep Paxton in check. Do you want to talk about what happened to you?"

I closed my eyes and sucked in a breath. "Not really. I'd like to just put it behind me. You're going to tell me I can't, aren't you?"

Harmony put a hand lightly on one of mine. "I'm going to tell you it's not that simple. You wouldn't have called in that favour if you had a choice. I've heard about this Dagen guy, he sounds like a nasty piece of work. And I know the kinds of things men do to have power over women. Taking away your ability to have children was as big a violation as forcing himself on you. Taking away your choice... It's evil."

"You're telling me," I said lightly. I didn't have any women friends, so this felt strange. Usually Jake and I just let each other rant and rave before we got back to work. It wasn't that he wasn't a good listener, but neither of us was very good at sharing deep feelings. Obviously, since it took us so long to get it together.

"He did… Other things?" Harmony asked gently. "You don't have to talk about it if you don't want to. Just know that if you do, I'm here for you." She gave me a funny look and then added, "The first time we met, I was terrified of you."

"If the next words out of your mouth are that you're not scared anymore, I'm going to be really pissed off," I said jokingly.

She laughed softly. "No, I'm still scared of you. But now I don't think you're going to have me killed."

"Not today," I agreed. "I think I'll save all of that for the black wolves."

"You're going to spill a lot of blood, aren't you?" she asked.

"A lot," I agreed. "I should have done it a long time ago. I was so busy trying not to provoke a war that I got myself caught up in a trap."

"Trying not to provoke a war is a good thing," she said. "Especially when you've got organisations like Zeta ready to step in and take advantage of any unrest."

"I should try to find a way to pit Zeta and Dagen

against each other," I mused. "Let them kill each other off."

"Please do," Harmony said with surprising enthusiasm. "That would take care of both our problems."

"I'll see what I can do," I said. If I could pull that off, it would be one hells of a move. And Harmony would owe me favours until the end of time.

I looked down at my knees. My heart raced and sweat spun up on my palms. If I was ever going to share this with anyone, it would be now. I couldn't imagine telling the guys, or even talking about it with Ben. The memory was too bitter, too raw. It always would be.

"My mouth," I whispered. Tears trickled down my cheeks.

"Your— Oh." My words must have taken a moment to register. "I'm so sorry. I should have blasted his helicopter out of the sky. It was either that or heal your friend Hutton. Paxton needed my help…"

She looked so apologetic, I found myself squeezing her hand.

"You made the right choice," I said. I would have said the same thing if Dagen had crashed and burned, literally. The past was the past. There was no point living in it. That said though, I was glad Hutton didn't die.

"This Dagen asshole must be really scared of you," she said. "If not before, then he should be now. I would be, if I did something like that to you. He tried to take away your power, but it didn't work. You're still just as badass as ever."

I wiped the tears off my cheeks. "You're right. That was exactly what he was trying to do, and he failed. And I'm going to make him hurt really, really badly. I'm glad you didn't destroy his helicopter. It would have been over much too quickly. He deserves to have his toenails and fingernails pulled out one by one. Literally and figuratively. And maybe every hair on his body as well."

Harmony grinned. "He deserves all of that and more. He's gonna really wish he hadn't crossed you."

"He certainly will," I agreed. "So will all of the men who work for him." Starting with the ones who held me down. "Every last one of them." I nodded with absolute certainty. "Thank you. It really did help to talk about it. But if you tell anyone what I told you, including Paxton, I will have you killed."

I wasn't joking now. No one else needed to know what happened. I would think about it this one last time, then never again. At least in theory.

Harmony smiled gently. "I would never tell anyone. You have my word on that. But if you ever want to talk about it a bit more, or about anything else, I'm happy to listen. Any time. I'll give you my number. As long as you can assure me it will never end up in Zeta's hands."

"It won't," I assured her. She was smart enough not to threaten me if it did, but I couldn't imagine any circumstances where I would give anything to Zeta other than a side eye and maybe a middle finger.

I also wasn't naïve enough to think this made Harmony and I friends. She was sweeter than I would ever be. Tough, but kind. Her children would grow up surrounded by love. If I'd had any children, they would have grown up surrounded by violence and blood. There was nothing wrong with those two things, but it wasn't the best environment for a child.

"The guys are probably itching to talk to you," she said. "They clearly adore you. Jake was beside himself when he contacted us. He tried to pretend he wasn't, but it was obvious. I don't think he slept in the last two weeks."

"Probably not, knowing Jake," I said. Now I felt a little bit bad because I had spent a lot of the last few days under the covers, fucking Ben. Not everything about the last two weeks was bad. Most of it, but not all of it.

"And Cooper," Harmony said as she got to her feet. "I'd be surprised if he doesn't walk along behind you, kissing the ground as you go." She laughed. "He's like a besotted puppy. Jake even calls him pup."

I didn't explain that it was short for Murder Pup, Jake's nickname for Cooper. Given to him because of Cooper's apparent fascination with murder.

"Cooper is very sweet," I agreed. He was certainly going to make an interesting assassin someday.

I stepped out the door and into Jake's arms.

"Were you listening?" I asked accusingly.

"Of course not," he said. "I was waiting patiently for you." He squeezed me like he had no intention of ever, ever letting go. He looked exhausted but he smelt like home.

I pressed my head against his chest and exhaled softly. "I wasn't sure if I would ever see you again."

"Of course you would," he said. "You can't get rid of me that easily. I would follow you to the bottom of the seven hells if I had to."

"So would I," Cooper said. He looked like he hadn't slept for two weeks either. He stepped over and gave us both a hug.

"Me too." Ben joined us on the other side.

Hutton cleared his throat.

When I looked over at him, he shrugged. "Just give me a chance? I did almost die for you."

Jake sighed loudly.

"Hutton did help us a lot," Cooper said. "Even you said so, Jake. We wouldn't have found her if it wasn't for him."

"You would have found me," I said. But it would have been too late for Ben. Too late for Hutton. Too late to prevent me from being violated further. Maybe too late to prevent me from being broken.

"Hutton did lead us right to you," Jake said grudgingly. "But I still want to reserve judgement until I see the rest of the information. And make sure there's not a virus in the message you sent."

"If there is, I didn't put it there," Hutton said.

"I can ask Freddie to have a look for you," Harmony said. "He's a genius with computers. If there's anything funny in there, he'll find it."

It was Jake who nodded. "I've heard that about him. I'll have our people look at it, but it wouldn't hurt to have a second set of eyes."

Harmony nodded. "Of course, he'll be happy to help. And if you meant what you said about pitting Dagen against Zeta, we'll help with that too."

"Anything to bring down those assholes," Paxton agreed.

I would have to see what they could do to help. I wasn't going to let their agenda get in the way of mine. My target was Dagen and the Onyx Ridge pack. Zeta would be collateral damage at best. They didn't need to know that though. They just needed to do what I asked when I asked them to do it. And they would, I would make sure of that.

10

"At least this place is still standing," I said as we pulled into the garage underneath Crimson. Jake pulled the SUV into the space beside my Cobra. "You drove her here?"

"I did," Cooper said. "Jake can't drive a manual."

Jake looked over his shoulder and scowled at Cooper. "I can drive one, I just let you drive that time because we had two cars and two of us." After a moment he admitted, "And if there was a bomb in the car, it would blow up Cooper, not me."

Cooper put a hand around his mouth and loudly whispered, "Jake can't drive a manual."

I knew very well Jake could, and this little display was just to cheer me up.

I managed a smile. "Maybe not, but it's always

sensible to let someone else drive a car that might explode."

"That's usually my job," Ben said. "Thanks for taking one for the team, Coop."

Cooper grinned. "Any time." His smile faded into a frown. "I don't actually want to get blown up though."

"Me either," Ben said. "The risk is just part of the job. It's what keeps it exciting." He gave me a faint smile and a nod. Exciting didn't accurately describe the last couple of weeks, but we got through it. More or less sane.

"I could use a bit of boredom for a while." I followed Ben out of the car and stepped over to inspect my Cobra. She didn't seem to be damaged, lucky for Cooper and Dagen. She was even parked inside the lines.

"These were still in there." Jake pulled out my phone and my mother's watch and handed them to me.

His fingers lingered on my palm and he locked his blue eyes on mine. "I thought about hiding that and getting you a smartwatch, but I figured you'd be pissed if I did."

I wasn't expecting the joke, so it took me a moment to realise what he was saying. When I did, I snorted and socked him lightly on the arm. "I like this watch. I took it off so it wouldn't get damaged when I shifted." I slipped it back onto my wrist and shoved my phone into the pocket of my skirt. There were probably a million messages on there. I would deal with those later.

"Thank you. I wasn't sure if I would see either of them again." Of course, they were just things. The watch and the Cobra had sentimental value, but at the end of the day they were replaceable. Like my phone.

Jake looked like he had something to say, probably plenty, but he took my hand and led me to the elevator. Cooper stayed close to me on the other side, and Hutton and Ben followed a couple of steps behind.

Through the bond, I felt Ben's tension rise slightly. That is to say, he was still the epitome of calm, but now he was on alert for any dangers. He was watching me and my every move, every step, looking for every possible risk on the way to the elevator. Inside the elevator. Inside the apartment as we stepped into the familiar space. Only once he'd walked around the apartment, looking carefully, did he relax slightly.

I wished I could relax. Being back here felt both

familiar and strange. Like nothing had happened, but everything had happened at the same time.

I walked over to the window and stood looking out at the view. Ferries and other boats slid across the shining water of the harbour. A cruise ship was moored at Circular Quay. Tiny people moved about, either getting ready to board, or disembarking from some adventure.

Life went on. A lot of the people out there would know who I was, but just as some rich nightclub owner. Not one of them would give a shit what happened to me. Plenty of them would probably think I deserved it. That I should be brought down to earth. And those were just the humans who had no idea shifters actually existed. A lot of the shifters who weren't wolves, had reason to dislike me. Just because Ivory Claw took better care of the city, and the state as a whole, than Dagen, didn't mean I wasn't part devil in their eyes.

Truthfully, I didn't really give a crap what they thought about me, as long as they stayed out of my way. I wasn't in this for the popularity. Still, it would be nice to know that if people were forced to take sides, I could be sure they would take mine.

"Elodie," Jake said softly.

I watched his reflection step up behind me. Tentatively, he put his hands on my shoulders.

"I'm fine," I said before he could speak. "Glad to be home. I assume there's a list of things I need to catch up on. I'll look at it in the morning. Unless there's anything you think I should see now." The last thing I wanted to do was think about work, but just as life went on, so did business. I couldn't afford to lose money because I was wallowing in self-pity.

"No, there's nothing urgent." He nestled his face into my shoulder. His breath brushed over my neck. "We've been taking care of things at the same time as we were looking for you. I figured you would growl at me if I let everything slide." His tone was light but I knew him better than to be fooled by it. He was obviously worried about me.

"Growl if you're lucky," I said. "Bite your head off if I came back to a total mess."

"Which head?" he asked teasingly.

I immediately stiffened. My breath caught in the back of my throat. The idea of his cock, anyone's cock, anywhere near my mouth…

Ben tensed in response to my sudden discomfort. Knowing he knew exactly why didn't make it any easier. I had to remind myself he'd also been through an ordeal. He'd almost died. He needed time, just like I did.

I mentally waved him down and forced myself to take a breath. "Either of them," I said, my voice more terse than I intended.

"Elodie, I'm sorry, I didn't—" Jake gently turned me around to face him. "I wasn't trying to pressure you." He locked his blue eyes on my brown ones. His emotions were written right there on his face. Including the thought that he failed me by not keeping me safe. As if he could watch me every hour of every day. As if Dagen wouldn't have taken us both and made Jake watch…

I swallowed. "I know you weren't," I said. "We wouldn't be us if we didn't joke around a bit. Right?"

He gave a slight shrug of one muscular, tattooed shoulder. "There's joking, and then there's saying things which upset you. I didn't mean to do that."

I knew he wasn't sure what he'd said wrong. That was half the problem. I couldn't really know what would set me off, and I wasn't ready to go into detail about what happened. I might never be. Too many people already knew for my comfort.

"I'm just tired," I said. "I'm sure we all are. It was a long drive back. You know me, I'm tough as nails unless I'm tired."

"I do know you," he said softly. "I know you'll keep everything bottled up inside if you can, because you're sure you can deal with it all by yourself."

"Because I *can* deal with it by myself," I said. "I'm a big girl, Jake, in case you hadn't noticed. I don't need you to hold my hand or fuss over me."

"Those are two of the things I do the best," he said. He gave me a boyish smile that made my heart flip.

"Maybe you need a new set of skills then," I snapped. I regretted the words the moment I said them. I stepped away from him and ran my hand through my hair.

"I'm sorry, I just—"

"Need an apple?" he asked, teasing gently.

"You and your fucking health food," I said, my tone lighter now. "Right now, I could use a big plate of bacon." I glanced at Ben before I added, "Cooked properly."

Ben smiled and nodded.

Jake didn't look impressed at being left out of an in-joke, but he forced a smile. "If you want bacon, I can send the Pup to get you some."

I resisted the urge to remind him that if I wanted bacon, I could send Cooper for it myself.

Cooper hopped up from where he was sitting on

the couch. "I can get us bacon. Maybe some eggs and toast. I know it's dinnertime but if that's what you want..."

I held back a sigh. Apparently he was going to fuss over me too. I appreciated the attention, but I wasn't made of glass. I wouldn't snap if they looked at me the wrong way.

I looked over at Hutton.

He shrugged. "I've never been very good at fussing over people. I'll leave that shit to these guys. If you want to know about the inner workings of the Onyx Ridge pack, I'm your dude. If you want me to go down on you, my tongue is all yours. I'll even go and get your bacon for you, but I guarantee I'll eat at least some of it on the way back. But fawning, just not my thing." He placed his hands behind his head and leaned against the back of the couch.

"Told you he was an asshole," Jake said. "Eating someone else's bacon is a new low." He pretended to glare at Hutton, but something had changed between them. It was more of a friendly rivalry than two men who hated each other.

Or maybe they were just being nice for my sake. Whatever. It was easier if they'd just got along anyway.

"I wasn't suggesting I eat your bacon, babe," Hutton said to me. "I'll happily eat Jake's."

"Is bacon a euphemism for genitals now?" Cooper asked.

Jake and Hutton both turned to stare at him. Ben started to laugh silently, but so hard he was soon doubled over, his palms pressed against his thighs.

Jake shook his head, but his momentary surprise and outrage soon turned to laughter as well. "It is now."

Hutton smirked. "If it is, then I retract what I said about Jake's." He looked at me. "But I'll definitely eat all of yours, babe."

I rolled my eyes at all of the guys. Was it possible for them to go more than five minutes without thinking about their dicks? Or my pussy?

I pulled out my phone. "I think I just order pizza." I looked at them all, challenging them to interpret that as some sort of innuendo.

"Hutton wants his with extra sausage," Jake said.

Yep, there it was. I should have seen that one coming.

"As long as it's not your sausage," Hutton retorted.

"I like mine spicy, like you," Cooper said to me. He gave me such an adoring look my heart almost melted on the spot. I didn't deserve anyone as fucking sweet as he was. He really was like a wolf pup at times. Naïve but also vicious. It didn't hurt that he was hot as hells and a quick learner in bed.

I pressed the buttons on the pizza restaurants app, and talked as I went. "Sausage for Hutton. Pepperoni for Cooper. Extra pineapple for Jake."

"Sick fuck," Hutton told Jake. The expression on his face was half grimace, half smile.

Jake shrugged. "It's healthier this way. Don't forget extra olives."

I added that to the order, plus meat lovers for me. I looked over to Ben, who had finally stopped laughing.

"Vegetarian with extra cheese, please, angel," he said.

I wasn't the only one who raised my eyebrows at the endearment. "I'm not sure I'm much of an angel," I said.

He smiled softly. "Yes you are. Very much so."

"One hundred percent accurate," Jake said firmly. "Right, Pup?"

"Right," Cooper agreed.

Even Hutton nodded.

"I can argue with one or two of you, but not all of you," I said. I pressed the button to complete the order and put my phone away. "I'll let you guys fight over who is going to go downstairs and meet the delivery person."

"Cooper and Ben can go," Jake said. "I'll keep an eye on you. You should be safe enough here."

"I'll keep an eye on you too, babe," Hutton said. "Can't trust a guy who has extra pineapple on his pizza."

"Can't trust a guy who keeps flirting with my woman," Jake retorted.

"It's up to her to decide whose woman she is, right babe?" Hutton said.

The testosterone in the room was off the charts. Usually, I liked it. Today it felt like a pressure on my chest.

"Just lay off each other," I snapped. "Or I'll kick you all out. After the pizza is delivered."

Both of them snapped their mouths shut so fast their teeth clicked. I wasn't sure if it was the threat of being kicked out, or the promise of missing out on pizza. Maybe both. Whatever, it got the desired result.

No one said being a wolf was easy. Especially when more than one of them wanted to be alpha. I needed to lay down the law more stringently, apparently. Jake got to play the role of alpha while we were in public, but I was the one in charge around here. They could argue amongst themselves about who was beta and who was omega, as long as they did what I told them to.

I sat down in one of the plush armchairs. Partly because I wanted to sit by myself and partly because the chair faced the rest of the room. I trusted all four of the guys with my life, but I couldn't sit with my back to them. I was going to be extra cautious for a while. A long while, probably.

No one would blame me for that. Frankly, fuck them if they did. I thought I was on guard before Dagen took me. I knew now that I wasn't on guard enough. I was distracted and let the asshole's mind games get to me. I had to be more focused than that. I had to be on my game every minute of every day.

Every second.

Jake knelt down in front of my chair, one hand on one arm, the other on his knee. "I didn't do enough to keep you safe, and I'm sorry for that. I expected Dagen to come after one of our businesses. I didn't think he would come after you personally. It's a ballsy move, especially for him."

"We should have anticipated every possibility," I said. "We took him by surprise by not being together. We should do that more often. Be apart. It wouldn't help the organisation if he takes us both out."

I sighed out my nose. "I was right, you know. About us being together. I thought we would be too distracted, and we were. It could have gotten one of us killed. Or both of us."

"El..." He looked like he was struggling to find the words to say. To deny the truth in what I was saying.

"I'm right and you know it," I said firmly.

"No, I don't know it," he said. "We weren't together because I was dealing with Haigwood, like I've dealt with a million things before. You drove yourself home like you've done at least as many times. Neither of us was any more or any less distracted than usual."

He closed his eyes for a moment and shook his head. "I remember what you said to me after you told me to contact Harmony. You told me you loved me. I know you, you don't say things like that unless you mean them."

"People say things when they're sure they're about to die," I said. Gods, my tone was colder than ice.

"Bullshit," he said. "I get it, you're freaked out. I don't know what Dagen did to you, but it obviously wasn't good. I wish you would confide in me, but if you feel like you can't..." He sucked in a breath. "Hells, Elodie, at least don't shut me out. We've been through too much together. You're my whole fucking universe." His voice was choked with emotion.

"I thought I lost you. Believe me when I tell you I just about ripped heaven and earth apart to find you. When I found your car parked by the side of the road and you not in it..." He swallowed audibly. "I could have ripped every black wolf in the state apart with my bare hands. I tortured a few for information. They're all dead now." He smiled fiercely. "They fucked with the wrong woman."

He turned one of my hands and laced his fingers into mine. "I think I've proved to you that I'll give you all the space you need. All the time. I'll do that again if I have to, for as long as it takes. Just, please don't keep me waiting for another eight years."

I bit my lip to keep from crying. I didn't need a bond to know how deeply he felt for me. I knew it since the day we met. I felt the same way.

But feeling vulnerable was worse than feeling lonely.

"Jake—"

He pressed a finger to my lips. "Don't tell me no.

Don't say anything. There's plenty of time for that. Let's just enjoy our pizza and that you're home with us again. We don't need to worry about anything else right now. Okay?"

I nodded and took his hand gently to move it away from my face. "I give you no guarantee I won't change my mind, but I shouldn't make a decision on an empty stomach."

Only, I already had made a decision. At some point he would have to accept it. He wouldn't like it, but it was how things had to be.

"Oh, fucking hells." I looked down at the corner of pizza which had dropped off my slice and slid down the front of my blouse. It left a long red smear, like blood, all the way down the fabric.

Jake chuckled. "You can't even blame me for that. It's not my fault this time."

"You look even more tasty," Cooper said.

I flashed Cooper a smile and flipped Jake the finger before picking up the corner and popping it in my mouth.

"I'm stuffed." I was surprised Jake let me eat as much as I wanted to without saying a word. Because of that, I ate an extra two pieces I didn't need and might regret later. Whatever, I didn't regret it now. I would have to work out twice as long in the morning, but I would welcome that to being locked in a room.

"I'm going to turn in," I said.

In unison, the guys all stood, like they were going to follow me into my bedroom. When they realised what they'd all done, they all stopped and looked at each other.

"Rock, paper, scissors?" Cooper asked.

"Alone," I said firmly. "The four of you can sort out the other two bedrooms and the couches. I need some time to myself."

Before they could argue with me, I turned and headed into my room. I closed the door behind me but didn't bother to lock it. If anyone got past the security and four guys, than a lock couldn't keep them out.

I dropped my clothes on the floor on the way to have a quick shower and pull on sleep shorts and a singlet. I half expected to find at least one of the guys waiting for me on or under the covers, but the room was empty. The bed was cold.

I pulled the covers up over myself and tried to get comfortable.

Ben sent reassuring thoughts through the bond and I sent him back assurances that I was fine.

While his special dose of calm was soothing, the

bond was disconcerting. Mostly, I didn't want him to know how I really felt. At best, he would worry about me. At worst, he would tell the other guys and they would start fussing over me all over again.

I should have asked Paxton and Harmony about the possibility of breaking the bond. Ben had a job to do, and this was another distraction that we didn't need.

I made a mental note to contact Harmony on the number she gave me and see if they could tell me how to break it. I couldn't imagine Ben wanted to be attached to me like this for the rest of his life. My mind was frenetic and chaotic. He didn't deserve to be inundated with that, constantly. He didn't mind now, but eventually he would. I was certain of it.

I lay awake for a long time, listening to the sounds of the guys' voices, and them settling down for the night.

Knowing Jake, he had a bedroom to himself. Cooper had all but moved into the third bedroom before I was taken. Hutton would probably sleep on the couch. Knowing Ben, he would stay awake all night watching over us all. The man was nothing if not diligent about doing his job.

I knew right now he thought of it as more than a job. I would have to remedy that. We formed a bond, aside from the magical one, because of our shared ordeal.

Now we were back, we had to return to being boss and bodyguard. Whether he liked it or not.

Whether *I* liked it or not. Letting myself get close to him was a mistake. I knew that now. We turned to each other because we were stuck in a horrible situation we weren't sure we would survive. I should have been tougher than that. I should have kept my distance. Easy to say when we were stuck in a room alone, but fucking him was unprofessional and stupid, and Dagen had taken full advantage of it.

In the back of my mind, I reminded myself that if we hadn't, I would have a bond with Dagen right now. And his slimy touch would have been all over my body.

I shuddered and pulled the covers tighter around me.

Here, alone in the dark, it was easy to let monsters crawl over, and under my skin. Memories I hid from when the guys were around found me here. Being held down. The surgery. The smell of blood before Dagen's wolves ate the parts of me he stole.

My stomach turned and the pizza threatened to come back up. I threw back the covers and staggered to the bathroom. I managed to hold back my hair and leaned over the toilet just before I lost every crumb of pizza, and then some.

I sank to my knees and waited until my stomach was completely empty before I rose and rinsed my mouth. I brushed my teeth and fled back to bed before any of the guys decided to check up on me.

Shit. I shouldn't have to worry about people caring about me. I was Ivory for gods' sake. People should be scared *of* me, not scared *for* me. And I certainly shouldn't feel like I needed to scurry around my own apartment above my own nightclub.

I pulled the covers back over myself and tried again to get comfortable. At least with my stomach purged, that was easier. I no longer felt bloated and stuffed. I just felt… Empty. Not just my stomach, but the rest of me as well.

Good. Empty was easier to deal with than vulnerable. Numb was a lot less painful. This was exactly the place I had retreated to after my parents' deaths. I built a wall of ice around me to shield myself from Helen Dagen and the rest of the Onyx Ridge pack. It got me through then, it would get me through now.

I closed my eyes and pushed everything away

until it was at arm's length, or further. The memories. The monsters. The guys. Everything.

No more crying. No more letting things get to me. The last thought I had before I dropped off to sleep was that I needed to build a frozen steel wall around my heart.

The empty feeling persisted when I woke an hour or two later. I was disoriented, but glad to be pulled from the dream I was having.

In it, was a girl of about four or five years old. She had white hair. At first, I thought she was me.

She turned to me with her big blue eyes and said, "Mummy?" Her resemblance to Jake and me knocked the breath out of my lungs.

"I'm not your mummy," I told her. "I can't be your mummy. Not ever."

She blinked slowly. More slowly than someone would in the waking world. "But why? Where is Daddy?" She looked around. We were home. Not at Crimson, but at my harbourside mansion. Me and her and Jake. And Cooper. And Ben. And Hutton. All of us, together. And this kid. This kid who couldn't exist, no matter how much I wanted to dream her into existence.

"Daddy?" she shouted. "Something is wrong with Mummy. She doesn't know who I am."

"It's..." I stammered. "I'm just pretending. Of course I know who you are."

She popped a hip and planted her fist against it in a pose must have learned from me. "Then what's my name?"

"I—"

I woke to the sound of an alarm. I sat up and rubbed my eyes. What the fuck?

The door opened and the light snapped on. Jake stepped inside wearing only boxer shorts. He had a phone to his ear.

Even half asleep and confused, I had to acknowledge how fucking hot he was. His body was a ripped tapestry of tattoos. Every bit of him was decorated muscle. I wanted to ignore the alarm, drag him down and fuck his brains out.

The sensible part of me realised it would be stupid to ignore an alarm. I pushed off the covers and grabbed a dressing gown to wind around myself.

"What is it?" I asked.

He frowned. "Apparently the building's sensors have detected a gas leak. We need to get out of here, just in case they're right." He waved at me to hurry up.

I nodded. If there was a gas leak, it would only

take a match, or a cigarette butt to take the whole building and us with it.

Hard pass on that, thank you.

"Let me guess, this has Alistair Dagen written all over it." He was probably pissed that we burnt down his country house. At least I assumed it burned down. The fire was looking fierce when we drove away. Whatever. That was firmly in the 'not my problem,' basket. This, on the other hand…

Jake followed me out into the sitting area just as Cooper appeared from his room. He rubbed his eyes and looked even more sleepy than I did. And just as painfully sexy as Jake. How was I supposed to keep my distance from these guys when they looked like they did? There should be a law or something.

Oh yeah, there probably was and they, being criminals like me, broke it.

*Men.*

Hutton either slept with his clothes on, or had dressed really quickly. Either way, he had everything on but his shoes. And you guessed it, he was no less sexy than Jake or Cooper.

Neither was Ben, who was the only one who was fully dressed, including his shoes. He was also the only one who actually looked awake and alert.

"We'll have to go down the stairs," Ben said. "The

elevators go off-line during an emergency like this. Just in case."

"Right," Jake agreed. "We don't want anyone getting stuck in there."

I assumed all of that was for Cooper and Hutton's benefit, because I knew all of that. Sometimes they seem to forget that I actually had a clue about what goes on in my own organisation. That was another thing I was going to have to remedy.

I lifted my chin and marched past them all to the door leading down to the stairs. At times like this being on the tenth floor sucked. I couldn't even cheer myself up with the idea that I would burn off all the pizza I ate. That was long gone.

"I should go first," Ben said. "To make sure it's safe."

It took me a moment to realise he was right. It was, after all, his job. This was not a time to let pride get in the way.

I nodded. "You and Cooper go first. Jake and Hutton, you two follow me. Keep your eyes and ears open. If there is a gas leak, it could be dangerous. If there isn't, then some other shit is up." Something that probably involved a pack of black wolves and a whole lot of fuck nope.

We trotted down the stairs in virtual silence.

Ben's shoes had rubber soles, so they didn't make a sound as we moved. Of course they did, he wouldn't be much of a bodyguard if he banged around as he went.

I kept my senses open and tried to keep my eyes from absorbing the sight of Cooper's bare back. Like the rest of him, it was rippling muscle. Absolutely ridiculously lickable muscle.

Shit, I had to stop thinking like this. It was not doing me or them any good. I reminded myself of my frozen steel wall. This was not a good time to be distracted.

"You okay, babe?" Hutton whispered. "You look pale."

I glanced back over my shoulder. "I'm fine. I could have used a few more hours of sleep, that's all." I realised he identified my growing panic before I did.

Judging by the way he glanced back at me, Ben did too. As ever, he was an island of calm in the middle of my chaos. He was focused on his job, but he allowed himself to take a moment to be concerned about me.

I gave him a look that reminded him once again that I could take care of myself. He gave me a minute nod and turned back towards the stairs in front of him.

"Couldn't we all?" Hutton said lightly.

I stopped mid-step. "Is he planning something? You would have a better idea of that than any of us."

"I wish I could say no," Hutton said. "But I remember something like this happening before. It didn't end well. We should get the hells out of the building." Now he looked pale.

I nodded and resumed trotting, faster than before.

We reached the fifth floor without seeing anyone else. From there, the stairs got busy. Floors four and five housed the brothel.

Sex workers were ushering clients out the door and down the stairwell. Some of the clients were in an obvious hurry to save themselves, but others seemed more concerned with their reputations. I recognised a couple of businessmen and local politicians. Being seen here would be damaging for them, to say the least.

Boo fucking hoo. They made that choice when they walked through the door. Curious how one or two who preached about 'family values' ended up here. They were hypocrites, but their money was as good as the next person's.

One of them noticed me and looked like he was ready to drop back behind me in the hope that any press who might be waiting outside would focus on me and not notice them.

They apparently changed their minds when Cooper and Ben ushered them forward. There was no way they would let anyone leave behind us. Or rather, they wanted to keep everyone in sight. It was never a good idea to turn your back on men like these, even though most of them were only human.

Only a couple of people stepped out of the doors at the third and second levels. By the time we reached the ground floor, the bar was empty.

I made a mental note to upgrade the evacuation procedures for the brothel. They should have been long gone before we got down there.

"You'd think the fear of dying would be greater than the fear of getting caught with your pants down," Jake remarked.

"When you build a house of cards on your reputation, then you have to be careful which way the wind blows," Hutton said.

"That's deep," Jake said. "Did you read that in a fortune cookie?"

"If you don't stop it, I'll have you both made into fortune cookies," I growled. "Hutton is right. Our clients rely on our discretion. That's why they come here and not somewhere else. And why they go out the side entrance while we go out the front." It would take us another minute, but it would keep our reputation intact.

That might be all Dagen planned, embarrass our clients into being too scared to come back. That would be bad for business.

Apparently the clients in question heard the words 'side entrance,' because they started to move faster. They followed the employees to the small door which led to an alley behind Crimson. From there, they would have to make their own way away from the area.

We headed across the wide foyer, out the large front doors and onto the street. Only a handful of staff stood outside. Our customers had dispersed, no doubt in a hurry to get as far away from a potential explosion as they could.

"Would you really have them made into fortune cookies?" Cooper asked.

I thought he was serious until he broke into a grin. "Why? Do you want to kill them for me?" I kept my voice low, in case anyone was listening.

His eyes widened. The conflict going on in his brain was obvious and kind of adorable. He wanted to say he would if I asked him to, but he wouldn't want to kill Jake. And he probably wouldn't want to kill Hutton.

I put him out of his misery before he had to answer. "I wouldn't ask you to do that. Besides, I don't think either of them would make very tasty cookies. Burgers, maybe." In spite of my empty stomach, the idea of food made me feel sick again.

"Now I'm hungry for a burger," Cooper sighed sadly.

"How do you have room for more food?" Hutton asked him. "You ate half the pizza."

Cooper shrugged. "I'm a growing boy."

"You will be growing if you keep eating like that," Hutton agreed.

Cooper, being the mature almost-twenty year old he was, stuck his tongue out at Hutton. "Don't worry about me. I'll work it off. Right, Ivory?"

I didn't have the heart to correct him right now, so I turned my attention to Ben. He was scanning the area, his eagle eyes taking in everything.

"Is anything out of place?" I asked. "Apart from us."

"Yeah, something," he agreed. "I can't quite put my finger on it. I would suggest we're being watched, but there are security cameras everywhere. Chances are, some of them aren't ours. Or aren't in our control."

"He does like to watch," I said. If I knew which cameras he might be watching us from, I would flip him the finger.

"There's no smell of gas," Ben pointed out.

I nodded slowly. "I noticed that too. Why get us out here then?"

He scanned the buildings around us, and the sky. "And how?" he asked. When I looked at him questioningly, he added, "The building's sensors were triggered by something. Or someone. Either from inside the building or remotely."

"Right," I said slowly. I didn't like either prospect. Either someone at Crimson was working for Dagen, or he'd found a weakness in our security system.

"Or he got us out here so we can see that." Jake sounded furious.

I turned and followed his gaze. "Fuck."

My restaurant, Scarlett, was on fire.

"MOTHER FUCKING son of a dingo's balls," I swore. "Couldn't he have sent a text message?" As if that would have been *so* much better.

Wailing sirens headed towards us. They echoed through the streets for a good two to three minutes before the fire trucks swung around the corner and stopped outside the restaurant.

Jake still had his phone to his ear. "Yeah, well, get someone out here. If there is really a gas leak… Yeah, well, hurry up." He hung up the phone and scowled. "Fucking gas company. If they worked for us I would fire them all. By the time they get someone out here to check, the whole place could have gone up. If that happened it would take the whole fucking block with it."

By now we all knew the gas leak was a load of bullshit, but he was right to be pissed off. If Crimson was flammable, we would all be incinerated.

"Gas leaks seem to follow you."

I was so busy watching the flames pour out of the front windows of my restaurant, I didn't see Singh or Gilbert approach until Singh spoke.

"Or is it just disaster?"

Unfortunately, that was a fair question.

I sighed. I was genuinely frustrated at the situation and confused why they were both still alive. Out of the corner of my eye, I caught Jake's expression. Apparently he was wondering the same thing. Or maybe he was just realising he'd forgotten to have them killed because he was so busy looking for me. Either way, he might end up in a hamburger patty yet.

"Like I said the last time we met," I said wearily, "people like me become targets. In the case of the gas leak, it seems to be a fault in the sensors. Hopefully that's all it is. I apologise for the disruption."

Crimson wasn't the only place evacuated. The area contained other restaurants, clubs and hotels. I didn't *need* their support or goodwill, but it was easier than having everyone around pissed off at us.

The hotels in particular sent a lot of customers our way.

"And the fire?" Singh said. "That is your restaurant, isn't it?"

"It is," I agreed. "Or it was anyway."

"So your restaurant catches fire on the same night that you may or may not have a gas leak in another one of your properties," Singh said slowly. "That sounds like an interesting coincidence to me."

I shrugged. "I guess that's your job to figure out if it was a coincidence or not. I'm not going to go around setting fire to my own restaurant, am I? It's not like I need the insurance money."

"You might have some other motive," she said. "You know anything about the disappearance of Jefferson Haigwood?" She was obviously trying to catch me off guard by the sudden change of topic. I was tired, but I wasn't going to be caught out that easily.

It was good to know some of the killings I ordered actually took place.

I cocked my head at them. "The owner of the Lair? I wasn't aware he had disappeared." That was true, it wasn't a disappearance. On the other hand, I actually *had* disappeared and apparently that went unnoticed by these assholes. They had their priorities inside out.

"He has," Singh said. "Hasn't been seen for about two weeks. You don't know anything about that, though, I suppose?"

"Not a thing," I said. I hadn't asked Jake or Cooper for any details, so it wasn't a lie. Not exactly. "Are you trying to accuse me of something?"

"Not at all," Singh said lightly.

Bullshit.

"It just seems coincidental that Silas Wheeler went missing, then Jefferson Haigwood. You get caught up in an explosion, then an apparent gas leak and now a restaurant fire." She gave me a hard look.

"If you're going to continue this line of conversation, we should continue in the presence of my lawyers," I said coldly. She was obviously trying to get a reaction out of me. Mentioning lawyers *was* a reaction, but the words were out now and I couldn't take them back. "Shouldn't you be down at my restaurant investigating the fire?"

"That's not our department," Gilbert said.

I had forgotten he was there until he spoke. Now I turned my gaze on him, I saw him mentally peeling off my dressing gown. He probably assumed I was naked underneath. I wanted to mentally peel off his skin and feed the rest of him to the wolves. Yeah, we don't always throw bodies in the harbour.

"What is your department?" I asked. "Harassing citizens in the middle of the night? Maybe you two triggered off the sensors?" Stranger things had been known to happen.

Gilbert chuckled. "It's not the kind of harassing I'd like to do in the middle of the night."

Singh and I both gave him twin looks of disgust.

"I think it's time you both left," I said. "If you have something to say, come back in the morning." Or better yet, don't come back at all.

Singh actually had the grace to look apologetic. Only for Gilbert. I saw on her face she was still certain I was up to something.

"I'd like to speak to your employee first," she said. She nodded towards Cooper. "He looked nervous when I mentioned Haigwood."

Cooper gaped at her, but had the sense to keep his mouth shut. His eyes flicked to me, obviously seeking guidance.

"His uncle disappeared, then Haigwood. You think the two are connected," I pointed out. "What are the chances whoever is behind this will come after him? That would scare anyone."

Cooper's eyes widened as if that was an actual possibility.

"Perhaps he can tell us," Singh said. "We'd like to talk to you. Away from her." She jerked her head towards me.

Cooper gaped again. "I—I guess so." He glanced at me.

I nodded.

Singh clearly thought I was giving him permission to talk to them. She thought I was arrogant, because the police didn't need my permission to speak to someone, but here I was, giving it.

Only I wasn't.

I was giving him permission to kill them. I preferred he not do it alone, but that couldn't be helped. I should have made up some shit about Hutton being our lawyer, or something, but it was too late for that.

"I'd offer you my office, but it might not be safe in there," I said helpfully.

I might send them into the building before we got the all clear, but not Cooper.

Also, he was about to make a big mess. I didn't want to have to replace the flooring. Again. Not in there, anyway. In other parts of the club, it was a frequent occurrence. Especially the third floor.

Cum stains could be so hard to get out of the carpet.

"We'll just step down this way," Singh said. She waved toward a spot in front of a lit window.

Cooper looked nervous, but excited.

Jake shook his head at him and smiled indulgently. Once the cops had moved away, he softly said, "Murder Pup. He really does get a kick out of that, doesn't he?"

"So do you," I pointed out. I could happily commit a bit of murder myself right now. "I want to see what's going on down at Scarlett." The firetrucks had been working there for quite some time and seemed to have the blaze under control. With any luck, it might not be as bad as I thought at first.

A girl could hope, right?

Jake nodded. "Ben, Hutton, go with her. I'll stay here and see if the gas company actually turns up."

He would also keep an eye on Cooper. The guy couldn't kill the cops in full view of everyone, so there might be a chance yet for someone to help him with the job. Better that than risking people hearing screams.

Things really started to get awkward then.

With the guys walking so close to me we almost touched, I headed down to Scarlett.

Two of the cleaners stood outside, both looking anxious. That anxiety rose when they saw me coming.

"Is everyone okay?" I asked.

"Yes, Ivory," one of them said. "It was only me and Leslie in there at the time." She cleared her throat. "I have no idea what happened. One minute I was cleaning the toilet, the next minute there was smoke everywhere."

Leslie nodded. "It didn't start in the kitchen. I was in there, cleaning the stove."

"Did you see anyone else around?" I asked. The police should be asking this. They probably would, later. Someone other than Singh and Gilbert. No doubt the fire department would also conduct an investigation to determine the cause of the fire.

Leslie shook her head. "No one. But..." She thought for a moment. "Now I think about it, I heard the back door open and close. I thought it was Jane, but then she came running from the bathroom area."

"So you got out through the front door?" I asked.

"Yeah," Jane said. "Just in time too. Something went woosh just after we stepped out." Her eyes were wide.

"I'm glad you got out," I said honestly. I had people whose job it was to die for me, these cleaners were not two of them. They were just staff on my payroll. People who didn't deserve to be dragged into Dagen's shit.

"Thank you, Ivory," Jane said. "Us too. Should we go or..."

I hesitated. "I think you should probably wait. Someone is going to turn up sooner or later with questions for you. Just answer honestly." Although both shifters, a tiger and a dingo, they would have little knowledge of the organisation they really worked for. It was unlikely they would say anything incriminating. Unfortunately, it was also unlikely they would say anything which would lead to Dagen being arrested or even blamed. Still, as long as it didn't lead to me, then it was what it was.

After a moment I added, "I'll find you both work at some other part of the organisation. Don't worry about that. And if you need some time off, take it. With full pay." It was the least I could do. They were almost burnt alive.

They both looked relieved at that.

"Thank you, Ivory," Jane said fervently. "I was freaking out. I can't afford to be off work."

I nodded to her. Okay, sometimes I forget there are people in the world like her. Lots of them. Most people weren't like me, with more money than they knew what to do with. Even growing up with Helen Dagen, I had everything I physically needed, and more.

That is to say, I always had a pair of shoes and a couple of changes of clothes. Helen was not what you would call generous, especially with me. She wasn't much nicer to her children, but she didn't raise a hand to any of *them*.

"And you won't be," I assured Jane. "You two do excellent work, I'd be crazy to let you get away."

Just as I finished speaking, another police car pulled up.

"Looks like the people who will want to talk to you." I stepped aside from the two cleaners and gave the police space to do their job. No doubt they would want to talk to me at some point as well, but Jane and Leslie were actual witnesses.

"Are you sure you trust them, babe?" Hutton said in my ear. "They could be working for him."

I would have to find a way to encourage him to stop calling me babe. "They've been working for me for years. It's possible they had something to do with it, but I think they're genuine."

"I agree," Ben said. "That was a nice thing you did."

"Giving them time off with pay?" I asked. "It

seemed like the right thing to do." I looked up at him for a moment. "Is that what you need, too? Some time off to deal with all the things that happened to us?"

"No," he said quickly. "I'm fine. What about you? Will you take some time off?" He looked like he was giving me a challenge.

"Hells no," I said. "I don't have time to take time off. No more than I have already taken off."

"I wouldn't call that time off," he said gently. He looked like he was going to step towards me but stopped when I almost took a step back.

At least the bond was good for something. Reminding him that personal space was a thing. It was a thing neither of us had had much of recently. I needed to make sure I got some from time to time.

"He's right, you know," Hutton said. "We should all take some time off. We've been through stuff."

I forgot he was behind enemy lines for longer than Ben and me. I hadn't had a chance to talk to him about it yet.

In the meantime, I asked, "Do you need time off?"

"Naw." He waved a hand in the air. "I'm good. I've had nothing but time off for the last few years. I am a man of action. I need to have things to do. I prefer those things don't include getting mauled to death by black wolves, or being exploded following a gas leak, but I'll take what I can get."

"That's good, because those things are pretty much a part of the job," I said. "Right, Ben?"

Ben gave a quick tilt of his head. "That is accurate, yes. It's a tough job, but someone has to do it."

"Yeah, I'm sure fucking the boss is a really tough job," Hutton said dryly.

The side of Ben's mouth twitched, but he didn't dignify that comment with a response. He must know I was pulling away from all the guys and wouldn't appreciate him talking to Hutton about what went on between us.

Everything in the past had to stay there. End of story.

The firefighters started to pack up their hoses and step out of the ruins of Scarlett.

With a sigh, I walked towards the woman who seemed to be in charge. "Is it gutted?" I asked.

She turned to me. "Are you the owner?" When I nodded, she said, "It's extensively damaged. We won't know the full extent until it's cold enough to go through and assess. I would think you're looking at a complete gut and rebuild of the interior. Fortunately, the fire didn't spread to the buildings on either side and the exterior seems to be intact. Again, we'll hold a full inspection in the morning. In the meantime, no one is allowed in or out. We'll put up tape. You know how people are though, they'll try to go in anyway."

She gave me a meaningful look as if she fully expected me to duck under the tape the moment they drove away.

Fuck that. I had a nasty enough dose of smoke inhalation yesterday, I didn't need one today. Or was it tomorrow already? Whatever.

"I won't be going in there," I assured her. "I let my staff know to stay out. Thank you. I'll be sure to send a few vouchers along to the station once we're back up and running. You can all have a night out on me." I really was being a fairy godmother tonight, wasn't I? I would have to be careful of that, people might start to think I was nice.

She nodded. "I don't think any of us would turn that down. If you excuse me, we should get going." She glanced at Ben and Hutton, then climbed back into the fire truck.

"See, that's another difference between you and Dagen," Hutton said. "He would have had them killed because they didn't put out the fire before it started."

I snorted. "Yeah, he would. That's the sort of

asshole he is." That and so much more. So much, much more.

I ran a hand over my hair. No doubt I wouldn't be allowed to start the cleanup until after the fire investigation, and the insurance investigation. At this point, I just wanted to get started on the rebuild. Every day the restaurant was closed would cost me money. Just because I wasn't short of a dollar didn't mean I wanted to lose it. I didn't get rich by throwing it away.

I glanced over towards Crimson. Jake was pacing back and forth. Stalking, really. One man, by himself, dressed only in boxer shorts. A man I loved so much I would push him away along with the rest of them. For their own good.

"In the time it took the firefighters to arrive and put out the fire, the gas people still haven't arrived," Hutton observed.

I nodded. "I noticed that. Strange that a private company is less efficient than a government entity. It's usually the other way around."

"Maybe Dagen owns them," Ben said. "That would explain their inefficiency."

I snorted. "Yes, it would." I started back towards Crimson, keeping an eye out for Cooper or anything out of place. I had so many reasons to be on edge, I couldn't even figure out which it was right now. Maybe all of them all at once.

I reached Jake just as the gas company finally arrived.

"It's about fucking time," he snapped.

They gave him a look, but got out their equipment and headed into Crimson to check it out.

"Of course the place is clear," Jake said. "What did they fucking expect? They'll probably send us a bill for coming out."

"And we'll pay it," I said calmly. I sipped my water and leaned against the back of the couch. They gave us the all clear an hour ago. Only the five of us, the cleaners and a handful of sex workers came back in.

Cooper's hair was still damp from the shower he had to wash all the blood from his skin. He hadn't stopped smiling since he reappeared from wherever he took the cops.

Jake muttered something and went on pacing. He'd pulled on a pair of worn jeans over his boxer shorts, but the rest of him was bare.

I tried my hardest not to appreciate the view.

I looked over to Ben, who was stretched out on the other couch, sleeping lightly. His head lay at an uncomfortable angle that would probably hurt later. I didn't have the heart to move him, in case he woke. It was almost dawn and he had been up for twenty-four hours.

Hutton and Cooper sat in chairs opposite each other and watched Jake stalk back and forth across the room.

"The security cameras near Scarlett just *happened* to be broken last night," I said. "Asshole must have planned this in advance."

Jake stopped and looked over at me. He snapped his fingers. "You're right. Accessing Crimson's sensors remotely wasn't something he thought up at the last second. Or if it was, he wouldn't have been able to pull it off that quickly."

"So he might have had access for a while," I said slowly. I resisted the reflex to look around the room. There were no cameras in my apartment. Not that I knew of anyway. If Jake put them in without my knowledge…

"That's a cheerful thought," Hutton said dryly. He *did* glance around. "Any chance our private conversations were overheard?"

"No," Jake said firmly. "This place is clean unless

he snuck someone in with a listening device or some shit." After a moment he added, "Which is unlikely, but possible. And a very good reason I should get Ivory out of here." He looked toward me. "I'll take you home for a few days. You could use a break."

"Do I get any say in this?" I gave him my best 'I am not amused' face.

"No," he replied lightly. "The whole building was evacuated and Scarlett is a burnt out ruin. The gods know what he'll pull next. He's trying to get to you." He hesitated for a moment. "He kept you both alive for a reason."

I closed my eyes and scrunched up my face. I didn't particularly want to talk about Dagen, but this was a conversation we needed to have.

"He wanted me to hand over everything to him. Just... Sign it over. He thought he would break me until I did what he wanted." I opened my eyes and exhaled out my nose. "I think that's what this was. He's trying to make me crack."

Jake looked disbelieving. "He just wanted you to sign all of Ivory Claw's assets over to him? Did he have any idea that's impossible?"

"I thought it was best not to let him know," I said. "He would have gone after you even harder."

Cooper looked confused. "Why is it impossible?"

Jake looked over at him, then glanced at Hutton. His jaw twitched. "In order to make any big decisions, any documents have to have three signatures on them. Mine, Ivory's and a third-party we keep tightly under wraps for just this reason. She couldn't sign anything over if she wanted to. Neither could I." He ran a hand over his head. "It's probably just as well he didn't know that. He probably would have killed you and declared war on the rest of us."

I placed my empty water glass on the table in front of me. "Another very good reason for me not to tell him. But what he did is as good as declaring war on us. So as far as I'm concerned, game on."

"After you take a few days off," Jake said firmly. "You can get dressed, or I'll *take* you like that." It was obvious by the way he emphasised the word, that he had more on his mind than driving me to my house.

"Is this where you'll throw me over your shoulder and carry me all the way if I try to refuse?" The idea was both aggravating and kinda hot at the same time.

"Yep," Jake said. He crossed his arms and gave me a look that was so fucking sexy it was unfair. I wanted to melt right into the couch.

And I wanted to run away and never looked

back. *For his own good,* I reminded myself. That was all.

I remembered the little girl in the dream. The only way he, or any of them, would be a father, was if they gave up on me and found other women. The idea hurt like a dagger to my heart, but it wasn't fair to them to wait around for me. Not when I knew I couldn't be with any of them.

"Fine. I'll get dressed." I stood and started towards my room.

"Need some help?" Cooper called out.

"No, I'm good." This time, I locked the door behind me. I knew without a shadow of a doubt at least one of them would follow me if I didn't.

I leaned against the door and sucked in a few shaky breaths.

Why was I more scared of my feelings than anything Dagen might do to me?

I could put it down to our growing war with the Onyx Ridge pack. Not only was I scared of being distracted, I was worried about getting so attached I couldn't deal with it if I lost any of them.

For the same reason, I needed to discourage their attachment to me. I had no plans to die anytime soon, but if I did, they needed to focus for the good of the organisation and every other white wolf in the state. The younger ones in particular.

I wanted them to grow up in a world where they didn't need to worry about shit like this.

I pressed my palms to the door and pushed myself off it.

With hurried steps, I walked to my wardrobe to get dressed and make myself a bit more presentable. It was almost dawn and I had an hour or two of sleep, but I didn't need to look like it.

Out of habit, I pulled a dress off a hanger. I paused and considered it for a moment. Low-cut in the front and the back, and with a long split in the thigh, it was exactly the kind of thing I liked to wear.

Today though, the idea of showing that much skin made me feel uncomfortable.

I chewed my lip for a moment.

This was exactly the kind of mind fuck Dagen got a kick out of. Making me feel vulnerable. Making me feel like I should wear a turtleneck and a skirt that fell to my ankles.

"Fuck you," I whispered. I didn't wear dresses like this because I like to be looked at. I wore them because I liked the way I felt in them. I would not be made to feel ashamed of the way I looked or dressed. I wouldn't hide, because if I did, then he won.

I slipped into the dress and looked at my reflection in the long mirror that hung on the wall.

"Yep, you're still a smoke show," I told myself. In a shade of deep red, the dress clung to my curves, flattering me to perfection. It fell to just above my ankles, but the split showed most of my right leg.

I'm not going to say I didn't feel a moment of self-consciousness. I did. I almost considered taking the dress off and putting on a skirt and blouse. And buttoning the blouse all the way up to my throat. And maybe throwing one of those wearable blankets over the top of the outfit. That would hide me.

Unfortunately I didn't own a wearable blanket anyway, so the dress would have to do. I brushed my hair and pushed my feet into a pair of heels. To the casual observer, I was still Ivory, the big bad she wolf. The woman who held influence over almost every corner of the state.

If you looked more closely, you might see a hint of Elodie, the woman who was struggling to keep all of it together.

I made another mental note. This time it was to have Jake contact all of the members of the wolves' conclave. Consisting of the alphas of each state of Australia, it was an uneasy alliance at best. We rarely met. When we did, it was because of situations like this. When one group was trying to overthrow another.

White wolves held sway in Western Australia and Tasmania. Black wolves lead Victoria and South Australia. Of course, Queensland had to be different, so their alphas were grey wolves. They tended to be neutral, so they would either stay out of it or try to mediate.

The Northern Territory, just to be really different, was led by a pack of dingoes.

The Western Australian and Tasmanian packs would send wolves if this turned into full-blown war.

South Australia wouldn't bother to return my messages. The dingoes would stay out of the way of all of us.

It was the Ironhide pack of Victoria I was the most interested in. They were led by Kian Quinn, with some help from his brothers, Tyler and Reed. Although as ruthless as the average black wolf, they tended to be more reasonable than the Onyx Ridge assholes. Kian might not help me directly, but he was proud of his reputation and that of black wolves in general. He may do nothing, but he might also send someone to assassinate Alistair Dagen.

If he could get a moment's break from trying to

stop his brothers from seducing every woman in sight. Including me.

My taste didn't usually run to black wolves, but Reed Quinn could do some pretty amazing things with his tongue.

What? Even I had moments of weakness.

I grabbed my phone and unlocked the door. The moment I opened it, I wished I'd gone for the turtle-neck and long skirt.

Four sets of eyes turned to drink in the sight of me. Blue, hazel and two sets of brown, they all had the same hungry look in them.

Hungry like the wolf.

Maybe I could go for one more round with all four of them, right here right now. Imagine the amount of orgasms I could have.

I swallowed and pushed away the thought as hard as I could.

Ben felt it, I saw it on his face. And then, of course, he was worried about me.

Fucking bond. The sooner I got the thing broken, the better. I would make that phone call when I got home to my place.

"Wow," Cooper said, open admiration on his face. "You look hot."

"Yeah, babe," Hutton said. "Fuck me upside down, you're gorgeous."

"I'm also the boss," I said coolly. "Something you all seem to have forgotten. Close your mouths."

Four sets of jaws snapped shut.

"Ben," I continued smoothly, "get some rest. You too, Hutton. Cooper, I'm sure Jake has assigned you duties? Good, make sure they're done. Are you coming, Jake?" Without waiting for a response, I swept towards the elevator.

I knew they were exchanging glances behind my back. Let them. They were my employees and I had overstepped with them. That changed as of now.

"Um, okay boss." Jake hurried after me. While I was getting ready he had taken some time to pull on a faded grey T-shirt. He might have even washed his face.

Sometimes I envied guys. Although there was nothing to stop me from wearing jeans and T-shirts and having my hair cut short. Nothing except I wouldn't feel like me. What can I say? Once a high strung, high maintenance girl, always a high strung, high maintenance girl.

"Are you okay, El?" he asked after the elevator doors slid shut.

"I'm about the same as the last hundred times people asked me that," I snapped.

I sighed and held up a hand before he could respond. "I'm fine. No, I'm not fine. I will be fine when Alistair Dagen is dead, and all of his shitty henchholes with him. Can you dig me a shallow grave for them? I'll dance on it."

"If you want a shallow grave for them, then a shallow grave is what you get," Jake said. "Just say the word. I'll organise the pack and we'll go after him tonight if you want."

"You know where he is?" I asked.

He sighed in frustration. "No, not as of this exact moment. If I had to guess, I would say he's not far away. He would want to keep an eye on the shit he is pulling. You know what they say about people always returning to the scene of the crime."

"Isn't that just on TV?" I asked. I had never gone back to any of the places where I killed people personally. But then again, the place where Helen Dagen's house once stood is now a women and children's crisis centre. The land was donated by an 'anonymous benefactor.' Every year, I send them funds to keep operating. It was a pet project of mine, so to speak, designed to help families stay together and away from abuse.

Jake shrugged. "I don't know. I've never gotten very far away from the scenes of mine."

"I suppose that's true." I watched him in the corner of my eye. "Maybe you should. You could take a break too, when all of this is over. Go to Tasmania for a holiday, or something."

He put a hand on my cheek and turned me to face him. "Don't."

I tried to keep from flinching. "Don't what?"

"Don't do that whole, 'go off and meet a nice girl' thing. We had that conversation before. You know I'm not going anywhere. I don't want anyone else."

"You know what he did to me," I said. I told him about the surgery during the drive. That was all though. I couldn't bring myself to mention what happened in the bathhouse. None of it.

"I can't have children. If you ever want—"

He cut me off with a loud laugh. "Me? A father? That's the funniest thing I've heard all month. No, really, it's been a shit month."

"You don't say," I said dryly.

He lightly pressed his forehead against mine. "If children were something you wanted, or if it happened, I would roll with it. If that was what it took to make you happy, then I would do it. But it's not something I want. Our world is crazy and you already have an heir to pass all of this down to. Assuming she has children."

Even when we were alone, I felt uncomfortable talking about her. As the last signee on any hand over documents, I tried to keep her existence a secret from everyone. I assumed Dagen had no idea I had a sister.

Well, half sister. Daughter of one of my father's lovers, we had different mothers. Different lives. We met in secret, for her safety, but she knew all about the organisation. She would only step in when my body and Jake's were both cold.

"She will. She is much more maternal than I am. Maybe you and her…"

He shook his head, making his skin roll lightly over mine. "Don't even go there. She's cute, but she's not you."

"But you admit she's cute." I pulled my face away from his and raised an eyebrow at him.

He looked up and around. "We probably shouldn't be talking about any of that in here."

"You're right," I said. "Your private life is your business."

"Elodie—" He exhaled in frustration. "I am never, ever going to give up on you. You can try to push me away but I'm not going."

"I'm damaged," I said, my voice tight. "You deserve better."

"No I don't," he said with a slow, self deprecating smile. "But the truth is, there is no better than you. As much as you don't want to believe it."

"Not for a minute," I agreed. Especially now. The truth is, I've always been damaged. For a long, long time. Sometimes it's an asset, because you can justify the horrible things you do by remembering the horrible things other people have done to you.

And sometimes, you just feel like shit.

"I know he did things to you," Jake said carefully. "I know you don't want to talk about it. But it doesn't change how I feel about you."

"It changes how I feel about myself," I admitted. "It made me realise I was right to avoid getting involved. It's the best thing for everyone."

"Don't you think I should have a say in what's best for me?" he asked.

"Of course," I agreed. "But I can't be part of that equation." No matter how much I desperately wanted him to hold me and kiss me right now. He was always so good at fighting off my monsters. Monsters except for Alistair Dagen. He was one I would have to take care of myself.

The elevator pinged and I stepped out on the

ground floor. My phone beeped a moment later. I pulled it out and looked at the screen.

"Fucking hells."

14

"Fucking peak hour traffic," Jake grumbled. He held down the horn for a few seconds. The sound made me wince. "That's a green light, dickhead."

He changed lanes in front of another car. When that driver honked his horn, Jake stuck his hand out the window and flipped him off.

"It's nice to see you don't give in to road rage," I said dryly. It was a welcome distraction, albeit a temporary one.

He snorted. "It's not road rage until I start ramming some motherfuckers. Which is going to happen really soon if these idiots don't get out of the way."

"Maybe you should get the car fitted with a

bazooka. Then you could just blast them all off the road." I pushed my sunglasses back up my nose.

"Trust me, I've thought about it." He pressed the horn again. "Or having it fitted with legs that elevate the car so high I can just drive over them. Better yet, we should have brought the helicopter."

"Under the circumstances, I think it's just as well we didn't," I said. "We might not have anywhere to land when we get there."

"You're right," he admitted. "This is still bullshit."

"Yeah." I leaned my head against the back of the seat behind me, but kept my eyes open. Every time I saw a black SUV, my heart raced. If I saw two of them within a kilometre or so of each other, my palms broke out in a sweat.

Every time, they turned off into sidestreets, or driveways, but I watched closely until they were out of sight.

"Are you…" He cleared his throat. "Sorry."

"If the next words out of your mouth was going to be 'in the mood for vanilla ice cream,' then yes," I replied. "I'll settle for banana ice cream too. A big bowl of it."

"Yes, that's totally what I was going to say," he lied. "How did you guess?"

"If you know me as well as you say you do, then you know when I need ice cream," I said.

"I do know," he said. "That's why I keep those apples around. They should satisfy sugar cravings."

I shook my head and didn't deign to answer. We were almost at my street anyway.

We went through another light and around a corner. There we were confronted with a couple of firetrucks, a few police cars and an ambulance.

"Looks like a murder scene," Jake muttered.

I sighed. "I wish it was a murder scene." I undid my seatbelt and was out of the car half a second after it stopped moving. I waited for Jake to catch up before I slipped between the emergency vehicles and stood gaping at my house.

It was still there, small mercies for that. Unfortunately it was also leaning right over a massive sinkhole which had opened between the foundation and the boundary fence. How lucky my neighbours were that it just *happened* to stop on my property.

"Fuck," I said breathlessly. "I give him points for being original, but bloody hells. The whole house might as well be gone."

"Is this your house, Miss?" A young police officer addressed me. Or to be more specific, my chest. She was pretty, with dark hair and blue eyes. It would be a shame if I had to kill her for annoying me right now.

"Not for much longer, by the looks of it," I said.

She looked up at my face and blushed. "The firies said they called an engineer. They might be able to shore it up. It's possible they could save it." She looked uncertain about that. "At least they might be able to make it safe so you could go in and get your valuables. Luckily, it doesn't seem to be a danger to the other houses in the area."

"Well, that's some consolation," I said dryly.

Her eyes widened and she looked like she was about to stammer out an apology.

"It is definitely a consolation for her neighbours," Jake said quickly. "I'm sure they'll appreciate it." Apparently he had worked off his aggression on the road, because he was congenial now.

"Of course it is," I said from behind gritted teeth.

She gave him a grateful look, which lingered longer than it should have, before she turned and walked away.

I shook my head at her back.

"She's just doing her job," Jake said.

"Like the gas company last night?" I asked sweetly. I knew I pressed just the right button when he scowled.

"Useless bloody..." He muttered something under his breath.

I wandered over to the curb on the other side of the street and sat down.

The sinkhole was obviously made by magic from Dagen's witch. I made yet another mental note. Get a siphon stone and have someone take her magic before I killed her slowly.

I drew in my legs because the whole street didn't need to see my ass in a g string. I looked over at my teetering house and sighed.

I remembered the day so long ago when I came home from school to find blood all over the house. Four men, all black wolves, stood in the kitchen. Damp hair suggested they had all recently had showers. Coffee and plates of sandwiches suggested they'd been there for a while.

Waiting for me.

I stood with my schoolbag over one shoulder and waited calmly for them to kill me. To this day, I don't know why I didn't run. Perhaps on some level I knew they weren't going to kill me. Honestly, I don't know why they didn't. It would have saved the pack a lot of hassle and death. I guess by sparing the daughter of the alphas, they thought they wouldn't look quite so bad.

"She looks like fun," one of them said.

Another gave him a funny look. "She's a kid."

The first black wolf shrugged. "I meant for hunting, not fucking, but we have our orders. Come on, kid." He downed the last of his coffee and jerked his head towards the door.

I hesitated, then lowered my bag to the floor. Without a word, I followed them past the table where my parents' heads sat, and out to a waiting vehicle.

"A million dollars for your thoughts." Jake sat down next to me.

"I'm just thinking I should have strangled Alistair Dagen when I had the chance," I said.

"When did you get a chance?" he asked.

I shrugged. "I didn't. But I still could have found a way, or at least tried." Maybe if I'd pretended to break, or pretended I wanted to spread my legs for him, I might have had a chance to be alone with him.

It was silly to even think it. There was no way I would have been anything but alone with him and several of his goons. The moment my hands went anywhere near his neck, they would be all over me.

I suppressed a shudder.

"That looks bad," Cooper said as he sat down on the other side of me.

I turned slowly and gave him a long look. "What are you doing here?" That was before I noticed Hutton standing behind me, rather than resting like I told him to.

"You said I should do whatever Jake told me to do," Cooper said. "He said to stay close behind you. He did say I should try not to let you see me, but I figured—" He nodded towards the house.

"It seemed like you could use some company," Hutton said. "Ben is keeping an eye on things at Crimson. And taking a nap."

Before I could say anything in response, the house shuddered. Dirt from around the edge of the sinkhole dislodged and fell. Dirt and foundations.

Fuck.

"Everyone back!" someone shouted.

The ground rumbled. Several windows shattered under the pressure. Seams in the brickwork started to come apart. The whole building listed heavily.

I wanted to close my eyes, cover my ears and pretend it wasn't happening. I could have gotten up and walked away. Come back when it was over.

Instead I rose, crossed my arms over my chest and watched my house tear itself apart and slide into the sinkhole.

Someone put an arm around me. I didn't register

who. I just leaned against him until there was nothing standing but a stubborn brick wall on the other end of the property.

"Well, shit," Hutton said. "That would have been cool if that wasn't your house."

"Yeah," I said absently. If anyone started with the 'at least no one was hurt,' bullshit, I was going to push them into the sinkhole myself.

My phone rang.

I put it to my ear, and barked, "What?"

I wasn't even slightly surprised to hear Alistair Dagen's voice on the other end of the line.

"I see you received my present," he said smoothly.

"Fuck you," I snarled.

"You seemed to enjoy doing just that," he said. "Shame you left so early. Think how much more fun you could have had."

I was tempted to throw my phone in the sinkhole.

"I hear your house burnt down," I said sweetly. "What a shame. It was so pretty out there."

Jake scowled when he realised who I was talking to. He mouthed that I should put the asshole on speaker phone, but I ignored him. Dagen was highly likely to say something I didn't want Jake to overhear.

"It was just one of many," Dagen said lightly. "No loss. Unlike your house. I understand your parents so tragically died there."

"You would know," I said. "Your parents killed them. But, like you, it's one of many properties I own. I could put two houses on this block and make a ton of money. I've been considering it, but you helped me make up my mind. Thank you so much." I wanted to pick up a brick and smash him in the face with it. Or better yet, in the balls.

The phone was silent for a moment. "I'm always happy to help out an old friend. Especially someone with such a warm, wet mouth."

I was ready for him to say something like that, but it still sent disgust snaking through my body and into my stomach. It reminded me I hadn't eaten since I threw up all that pizza. That was probably just as well. I might have vomited on the remains of my house.

Later, I would think of the perfect come back. Right now my brain was frazzled and blank.

All I said instead was, "We're not friends, asshole. In fact, why don't you come down to the harbour? There's a nice big hole right in front of me that I could throw you in. I'm sure no one will miss you."

"Maybe your hole wouldn't be so big if you weren't such a slut," he said.

Ouch. A burn and a slut shame rolled into one. This guy was pure class.

I laughed. "At least I don't have to pay for it." I was tempted to retort that at least I didn't have to have three men hold someone down for me, but the guys were right next to me.

"Perhaps, but I can father children," he said.

I could just picture the smug expression on his face.

He hit me right where he aimed, in the heart.

I managed another laugh. "Yes, you're one up on me. I can't father children. Funny though, because I'm pretty sure my cock is bigger than yours."

He chuckled. "Ah yes, my cock. I'm sure you dream about it at night. Do you remember how it felt when I squirted hot cum down your throat?"

I ended the call. I wanted to put the phone down on the ground and grind my heel into the screen. That would achieve nothing apart from breaking my phone. The hassle of replacing it outweighed the satisfaction I might get from destroying it.

I would get much more satisfaction from destroying Dagen.

My phone pinged with a text message. I almost ignored it.

I should have.

I glanced at the screen.

*You look sexy in that red dress.* Yeah, he actually ended the message with a full stop. What a monster.

"Motherfu—" I gripped my phone tight in my hand and looked around. My heart pounded like thunder. My palms were almost sweaty enough to drip.

"El? What is it?" Jake grabbed my wrist and turned it far enough to read the screen.

"He's here somewhere," I said. "He's watching me. Us. We need to find him."

Jake started to look around too. "I don't see anyone but the emergency crews, and…"

The neighbours were trickling out of their homes. They cast anxious glances at the empty lot where my house once stood.

"In a window?" I squinted, but light reflected off every window I saw.

"Um, babe," Hutton said.

I turned to him. "What? You see him?"

He shook his head. "No." He pointed toward a security camera directly opposite my wrecked house. "I'd guess he's watching through that."

"Fucking creep." I stuck up both middle fingers to the camera.

My phone pinged again.

*I look forward to breaking both of those. Right before I break you, bitch.*

Yep, I should have ignored him, but I wrote, *Don't call me bitch*, and hit send.

He responded a moment later with a laughing face emoji and a dog. A second later he added an eggplant, a donut and a panting, hot face.

"Ewww." I thought about replying with a clown or devil face, but he might think I was referring to myself.

"You know you can block him, right?" Cooper said. He sounded like a teenager explaining new technology to someone who prefers older technology…

Oh. Well, anyway, I grimaced at him. "He'd only change numbers and contact me again. He's a slug." And frankly I could have done without the mentions of what he did to me. I knew he was trying to get to me, but shit, it was working. I should be tougher than this.

I *was* tougher than this.

The street was now buzzing with people, including TV cameras and roving journalists. They seemed to be hunting for witnesses to talk about my house sinking into the earth.

Newsflash, I didn't want to talk about it.

"Let's get out of here." I glanced at Jake.

He sighed, but nodded. "Hutton, Cooper, you guys stay here and deal with any questions. Tell them you don't know anything, but you're authorised to liaise with the owner to organise the clean up. We'll do whatever the engineers recommend."

"You trust me, huh?" Hutton looked smug.

"Fuck no, but it's not safe for Ivory. You can't do too much damage here." Jake gave him a sarcastic smile, then put a possessive hand on my back to guide me to the car.

"Are you going to tell me I should try to trust him?" he asked as he opened the passenger side door.

I gave him a look for apparently assuming I suddenly lost the ability to open a car door. "At this point, I'm not sure I trust myself."

"As long as you trust me." He actually waited until I was sitting in the car before he closed the door and walked around the other side.

"Yeah, I might," I told him as he slipped into his seat. Part of me wanted to tell him to find a quiet street so I could fuck him in the back seat. It was long enough to comfortably fit us both. Jake did like luxury in all of his cars.

Then I remembered I was trying to keep my distance. And this was Sydney. Quiet streets were like virgins—hard to find, and harder to fuck in. Yeah, okay, that sounded better in my head.

"You can always trust me," he said, his blue eyes intent on my face. "You know that, right? Whatever happens, whatever or whoever you do, I will always be right there, ready to catch you."

Fuck, he had so much love in his tone it broke my heart a little. How was I supposed to keep my distance from him when he adored me as much as I adored him? We had tied our lives together a long time ago. Some knots couldn't be undone, even if they strangled us both.

"I don't plan on falling," I said softly. Literally, figuratively or in love. I knew he understood my triple meaning. I also knew he didn't buy it any more than I did.

Frozen steel, I reminded myself. Even if I ripped out my own heart in the process.

I don't know, maybe I had no heart. If I did, surely I wouldn't turn my back on someone who looked at me the way he did. Maybe I was a coward. I had never let anyone in fully, since I was a kid. I trusted people, sure, and that was a huge deal, but lowering all of my walls… That was something else entirely.

I supposed I fit the nickname Ice Bitch. I acknowledged long ago I wasn't a nice person. I was okay with that. I was a killer surrounded by killers. I was cold, sarcastic, composed, distant.

But when I looked back at him, a hidden part of my heart begged to melt. To let him in. To let Ben, Cooper and Hutton in. I was a crappy person, but even crappy people needed to be loved.

Except Dagen. He could fuck himself. But me—Ivory was damaged, but Elodie needed to be held, comforted and protected from the big, bad world.

Which side of me would win? I had no idea, but it was going to be an epic boss fight.

15

"A LOT of this is useful, if we can believe a word of it." Jake adjusted his reading glasses and pointed at the screen.

He hated wearing them. The fact that he was showed how much material Hutton sent. He either had to wear them, or he'd have a massive headache later.

"Dagen did let him back into the fold pretty quickly," he added.

"I don't think he bought Hutton's loyalty to him for a second," I admitted. "Letting him have access to that information was a test. Hutton failed." Or passed, depending on the criteria. I knew I could trust him. I should have known Dagen wasn't dumb enough to be fooled.

"So it's probably useless." Jake snatched his glasses off his face and rubbed the bridge of his nose between his thumb and forefinger. "A red herring to feed back to us."

"It's a very extensive red herring if it is," I pointed out. "We can actually confirm quite a bit of that ourselves. Either Hutton was going to pass the test or he was going to be killed. It's possible Dagen thought he had nothing to lose." No, I didn't buy that either. Alistair Dagen was not stupid. This would be a lot easier if he was.

I stopped pacing and sat on the side of the desk. "Somewhere in there is some kind of trap. Something that looks harmless, but when we look into it—"

"It will blow up in our faces. Get us killed," Jake finished for me.

"Killed if we're lucky." I drummed my nails on the desktop. "It's probably best to stop looking at it. Knowing him, it'll be something which would spark our curiosity."

"It wasn't just the cat that curiosity killed," Jake said. "But now I feel like we have a puzzle to solve. See if we can find the deadly clue hidden in the files."

"If you need something to hunt, I could throw you a ball," I said dryly.

He chuckled. "Would you? It's been a while since I've had that much fun. Maybe we could get one of those big, inflatable ones and go to the beach."

"Are we still talking about balls, or something else inflatable?" I teased.

He grinned. "It's not exactly the kind of three-some I have in mind." He ran the tip of his finger over the back of my hand. The touch made me shiver.

"Jake—"

He rose from his chair and moved to stand in front of me. He placed his hands on the desktop to either side of me.

"Shhh." He brought his lips to mine in a whisper soft kiss. It was barely a brush.

Heat flooded right to my core.

He pulled away and looked me in the eyes, conveying a thousand emotions in one glance.

I felt like I lived a hundred lifetimes in that brief moment. Then all of that disappeared when he slammed his mouth against mine.

Where the first kiss was soft and tender, this was fierce and possessive. The alpha wolf claiming what was his.

He snaked a hand around the back of my head.

His tongue dipped into my mouth, testing, tasting, running over my lips.

His other hand slid up the outside of my thigh, under my dress. He cupped my ass and gave it a squeeze.

I broke off the kiss. "Jake…"

"Shhh," he said again. He slid his hand from the back of my head, down my arm and onto my other thigh. Slowly, he sank to his knees. He pushed my thighs apart and rubbed the back of his knuckle against the gusset of my panties.

I bit my lip to hold back a groan. I was already panting at his touch.

And he was merciless.

He grabbed the front of my panties and literally tore them away. He gripped my thighs with firm fingers and vigourously attacked my pussy with his tongue. He licked me all the way from my clit to my rear hole.

He tickled that a time or two before focusing all of his attention on my clit and entrance.

I didn't bother to hold back a second groan. "That feels so good." We shouldn't have been doing this, but gods, I couldn't stop.

"It tastes so good," he said, his voice muffled by a

mouthful of pussy. "I want to feel you come on my face. But not yet."

If he kept doing what he was doing, I wouldn't be able to stop myself. And he did keep doing it. He dipped his tongue in and out of me, then stroked me from front to back, and back again.

I pressed my palms to the desktop for stability, and rocked lightly against his mouth. "Oh gods, I'm so close."

"Not yet," he said. He looked up at me and pulled back his mouth long enough to say, "Touch your breasts for me."

While he got busy with his mouth again, I unzipped my dress and slipped it down my shoulders. I unhooked my bra and placed it to one side on the desk. My nipples were already hard before I started to run the tips of my fingers around and over them.

"Good girl," he said.

For some reason, his words made me hotter than ever. "I need to come. Please."

His fingers gripped my thighs tighter. "Okay, Elodie. Come for me."

He licked me so hard it almost hurt, but I came hard, grinding my pussy against his mouth. The scratch of his stubble against my sensitive skin pushed me over the long, steep drop to blissful oblivion. My vision blurred. My mind knew nothing but pleasure.

I think I screamed his name, but all I knew was that my throat was raw afterwards.

I was only halfway down when he rose, and pulled me off the desk.

He grabbed a handful of fabric and jerked my dress the rest of the way off. With one hand, he turned me around and bent me over the top of the desk. With the other, he unzipped his jeans and pushed them down his hips.

I barely had any warning before he pounded his cock all the way inside me, from tip to balls.

I cried out in surprise. If I thought he would give me a moment to compose myself, or get used to the feeling of him inside me, I was wrong.

Just as his tongue was merciless, so was his cock. He pulled all the way out, then slammed back in, over and over. He was like an animal, asserting absolute control over his mate. Every bit of me was his and he would do whatever he wanted to me.

He slid a hand up my belly and cupped my breast. He gripped it hard enough to hurt, but at the same time it felt so good.

The moment his tongue touched my pussy, I had

relinquished every bit of control to him. It was hot and it was liberating. Just like when he and Cooper had both taken control and fucked me, I wanted more. I wanted him to dominate me.

I leaned my elbows on the desk and dropped my head almost to the wood. I spread my legs a little further apart to let him go in deeper.

"That's it," he said. "Perfect. Gods, Elodie, you feel so good." He ran the heel of his hand up and down my taut nipple. "So fucking good." Without warning, he pulled out of me. He turned me around, put his hands on hips and placed me back on the desk.

"Lie back." He grabbed my feet, and placed them on the top of the desk, so I was lying with my knees spread as far apart as they could go. He took a moment to admire the view, before he grabbed my ankles to keep me in place and drove himself back into my body.

He slid a hand between us and rubbed my clit.

I closed my eyes.

"No," he said. "Look at me. Watch me while I fuck you."

Holy shit, that was hot.

I opened my eyes, but had to pick up my head to see as much of him as I could. I propped myself up on my elbows and watched his chiselled torso move as he thrust in and out of my slick heat.

"It's the best view in the world, isn't it?" he asked.

"Billion-dollar view," I agreed. I had to admit I attracted some pretty hot guys.

He smiled and massaged my clit firmly with his thumb. "Come again," he ordered. "I know you can."

"Mmmm, I'm sure I can," I agreed. Between his thumb and the friction of his cock sliding back and forth across the most sensitive part of my body, I was close again.

"Of course you can, you know why?" he asked. "Because I told you to. And because when I fuck you, I am in charge."

There was something about those words that turned me on so hard. I moaned.

"You like to hear that?" he asked. He paused his thrusting and rubbed me harder. He leaned forward and whispered, "I'm the boss. Come for me again."

I came all right. Like thunder, lightning, fireworks and vanilla ice cream all rolled into one. Every nerve in my body lit up in a rush of heat, blood and pleasure. I cried out as the warmth rushed over me, from my toes to the top of my head.

He started to thrust again. After maybe a dozen

strokes, he came too, with a series of hard, animalistic grunts.

Finally he flopped forward, panting.

I lowered my legs so they hung off the side of the desk, and looked up at the ceiling.

*Fuck.*

*Fuck. Fuck. Fuck.*

I sat up so he slid out of me. I rubbed my forehead with my fingertips and exhaled. What was I thinking? Oh, right, I wasn't thinking.

"Jake…"

His head jerked up.

"I'm sorry. I should have— We shouldn't have done that," I said softly.

"Elodie—"

I swung my leg over and dropped to the floor. "I'm sorry. This was a mistake. I should have stopped it before it went this far."

The look on his face was like a stab to the heart. I guessed he assumed fucking meant we could move forward the way we were before Dagen took me. Or maybe he hoped it would convince me.

"Bullshit," he said after a moment of shocked silence. "Nothing about this was a mistake. I love you. I know you love me. You say you only said it because you were scared but I don't buy it, El. You wanted this as much as I did. Not just this." He waved at the desk top. *"Us."*

For the first time since we met, he looked like a lost boy. Like he was desperate to find the right words to fix this, but knew it was like putting a small bandage over a severed limb.

"Wanting something doesn't mean it's a good idea," I said coolly. I pushed all the walls I had lowered for the last hour or so back into place. "I don't want to lead you on. It's not fair to you."

He snorted and pulled his jeans back up. "I'm a big boy. I can decide for myself. I decided the moment I met you. I know for a fact you did too. I also know you feel the same way about the other guys. That's why you trusted them so quickly. It was because you knew there was something there. Something that binds you to them, the same way we are bound together. I know they feel the same way about you, even Hutton." He grimaced.

He put his hands on my shoulders and looked me in the eyes. "I know you've been through a lot—"

"Because I let my guard down," I said. "I can't do that again. Ever. Not with you and not with any of them. Not even with myself. It won't be the restaurant or my house next time. There is nothing he won't try to take from me to break me. How do you think I will feel if the next thing he takes is you? Or any of the guys? I can't..."

I swallowed down a knot of emotion. "I can't afford to be that vulnerable. The best, safest place for all of you is as far away from me as you can get. Let me deal with Dagen and—"

"If you think I am walking away from you *ever*, much less right now, you're out of your mind," he said. "Whether you like it or not, we are a team. We feel what we feel. We can't turn it off. I don't want to. I don't think this was a mistake. I will never, ever regret making love to you."

He dropped his hands and took a few steps away. He let out an exasperated sigh and turned back. "I wish I knew what I had to say or do to convince you."

I saw the sincerity in his eyes, heard it in his voice. If there was a single word or act he could say or do to convince me, he would say or do it.

I looked down at the floor, then back up again."There is nothing you can say or do. You know how stubborn I am."

"And you know how stubborn I am," he said. "I will die before I give up on you."

"You might die *because* you didn't give up on me," I told him.

He shrugged. "Then I die. But I would rather die by your side, fighting Dagen, or some other monster, than live without you."

He was nothing if not romantic.

I had no answer for him.

I crouched down to scoop up my dress off the floor. That was something I had always done. I hated to bend over, especially in front of other people. For some reason, it made me feel unbearably vulnerable. I frowned at the remains of my ruined panties. I held them up between my thumb and forefinger.

"Was that necessary?"

He grinned. "Absolutely. Yes. I'll buy you some new ones." Without missing a beat, he added, "I will tear those off as well."

He really wasn't going to give up, was he?

"At least I'm not covered in blood, juice or mud," I said. "For once." There might be a blade or two of grass on the back of my dress, but I decided not to look.

"I knew I should have come on your stomach," he said. "Next time."

It was just as well he hadn't. The idea of his cock even that close to my face made me want to shudder. I probably would have run away screaming. I had a panic attack...

Like I was starting to have right now…

His phone rang. I thought he was going to ignore it, but he glanced at the screen. "I should get that."

"Saved by the bell," I muttered.

I picked up my own phone and headed towards the apartment for a change of clothes. If either of the bodyguards standing outside the door were surprised to see me walk past naked, they gave no sign. Internally, I was a trembling mess, but this was another thing I refused to change just because I felt threatened by Dagen. What kind of shifter was modest anyway?

I padded silently past Ben, who was asleep on the couch. He stirred when I got close, which didn't surprise me. Between the bond and his vigilance, he probably knew I was there. Even in his sleep.

I threw on an old T-shirt and a pair of track pants. The kind of clothes I wore to work out in. I should go down to the gym and do that after I made this call.

I opened contacts and pressed on one of the names. It rang a couple of times before a male voice came on the line.

"Yes?" Paxton said. He must have recognised my number, because he asked, "Do you want to talk to Harmony?"

"No," I replied. "It's you I need to talk to." As briefly as I could, I explained the reason for my call.

"Yeah, that's something I can do. If you're sure."

"I'm very sure," I said. "It's the right thing to do. For everyone." I expected him to say something about not making decisions on behalf of other people, but he didn't.

Instead he said, "Is tomorrow okay?"

"It can wait until then," I said. I ended the call with all the usual niceties that neither of us were comfortable with.

"Anything wrong?" Jake asked.

I hadn't heard him come in, and I almost jumped out of my skin as a result. I turned around and tried not to look guilty. "Everything's fine. You? That call seemed important."

"You suggested I contact the conclave. That was Kian Quinn. He and his brothers will be up next week. The Tasmanian alphas have confirmed they are also coming. The grey wolves from Queensland left us on read." He shrugged. "I was thinking I should organise some extra 'entertainment' for Tyler and Reed Quinn, so they can let off steam when they get here." He rolled his eyes towards the ceiling. As if he wouldn't fuck me every chance he got.

Still, he had a point. The brothers did seem to be

insatiable. Jake's attempt to keep them away from me was about as transparent as a brick wall.

"Do you think I can't handle them?" I asked.

"I know you can handle them," he said. "But didn't you just say you didn't want any distractions?"

Trust him to turn my words back on me like that. He was right though. Tensions between white and black wolves were strained enough without me fucking a pair of them. Truthfully though, I wasn't even tempted. Why would I want burgers when I had perfectly cooked bacon I was trying to resist?

For a moment I thought about a burger with bacon piled on top of it, but I was probably getting greedy. Although, giving control to four guys…

Gods, when did my vagina become so needy? And how the fuck was I actually supposed to resist four, hot guys?

16

"COME IN." I stepped aside from the small side door of Crimson to let Paxton, Harmony and Jordan come inside.

Jordan, another one of Harmony's boyfriends, had almost as many tattoos as Jake. Like Jake, he looked like the sort of guy who would hurt you if you looked at him the wrong way.

I was certain he would hurt anyone who lay a hand on Harmony. The looks they exchanged clearly showed they adored each other. I hadn't met her other two guys, both Jordan's brothers, but Jordan and Paxton couldn't be much different.

I guessed that kept her life interesting.

Jordan gave me a measured look. "Thanks for helping us when Harmony needed to get her magic back. Sorry I couldn't be there to help rescue you. Kayden, our son, is going through a phase. He's a powerful witch. When he's being difficult, it's best to have someone around who can use magic."

"We wouldn't want magic to go awry," I said dryly. Personally, I would be okay with it not existing at all. Although, it did come in handy for healing. It was certainly more efficient than human medicine.

"We really wouldn't," Paxton agreed. "Fortunately, Harmony's sister was available to take care of him today. What you need us to do will take a lot of magic. I'll need all the help I can get."

Harmony hadn't said a word since she walked through the door, but she offered me a reassuring smile.

Confiding in her the other day helped at the time, but now… Now it was disconcerting knowing she knew what happened to me. She wouldn't tell anyone, but still, she knew.

"This way." I led them over to the elevator. It was a squeeze with me, three of them and two of my bodyguards. I didn't trust Harmony and her men enough to leave security behind.

I wasn't naïve; three wolves stood little chance

against three powerful witches, but it was better than taking them on alone.

"Nice view," Paxton said as he was ushered into my office on the tenth floor. "Who said crime doesn't pay?"

Harmony gave him a sharp look.

Jordan looked alarmed, but relaxed slightly when I smiled.

"The people who say that aren't doing it right," I said. "Fortunately, that's most people, or property prices in the area would be even higher than they are now."

I waved them towards the couches on the side of the room and pulled out my phone to send a text to Ben. I could have summoned him through the bond, but that was something neither of us should get used to.

He wasn't far anyway, just in my apartment looking around for hidden cameras or listening devices. He was certain he wouldn't find any, but insisted on looking anyway. It didn't hurt to be vigilant, and it kept him busy for a while.

He stepped through the doorway a couple of minutes later, followed by Cooper.

"Hey," Cooper greeted the newcomers warmly.

"Long time, no see." He offered his hand to Paxton and Harmony before introducing himself to Jordan.

All the while, Ben stood near the doorway. He looked composed but wary. He must have caught some inkling of what was going on. Finally, he moved over to stand beside me, almost close enough for our hands to touch.

I sensed he wanted to lace his fingers in mine, but he didn't.

"What's going on?" he asked softly.

"They're here to break the bond," I said as lightly as I could.

It took him a moment to realise what I said. Surprise and hurt crossed his face and flooded through the bond.

"Can we talk about this? Alone?" His eyes pleaded with me.

I thought about refusing, but I owed him that much. "Cooper, offer our guests a drink. Ben and I will be back in a minute."

I gestured towards the door and waited for him to walk through first before I followed.

He led me all the way to the apartment and closed the door behind us.

He turned to face me. "Do I get any say in this?"

Through the bond, I felt his need to reach out to

me. To hold me. Only his practiced restraint held him back.

"It's the best thing for you too," I said. "It's not healthy for you to be connected to me like this. It's only been a few days and I'm surprised you're not insane already." I was only half joking. "Or tired of me."

"You know how much I hate magic," he said softly. "But having the connection to you has been…" He searched for the right words. "Enlightening. Weird. Wonderful. Feeling you enjoy it when I touched you was… Fucking hot. It was a whole new level of intimacy."

"It was," I agreed. "But it's not appropriate between a boss and her employee."

He brushed his knuckles lightly over my cheek. "We're more than that. You know how I feel about you. I know how you feel about me. Even without the bond, we share something."

I wanted to melt into his touch. Let Cooper entertain our guests for an hour or two, while we entertained each other.

Instead, I stepped away from him.

"What we *had*. We have to forget about it. We're back home now. Things have to go back to the way they were."

"I can feel how hard you're trying to convince yourself of that," he said. "But I can also feel that you don't believe it either. I know you're trying to distance yourself from all four of us to protect yourself. And to protect us. But we're all big boys, we can protect ourselves. And you."

"The fact that you say all of that is another reason to break the bond," I said. "Do we really need to know what each other is thinking? Or feeling?" I shook my head. "It's not normal. If nothing else, women are supposed to be mysterious. The bond is fucking with that."

"You're still mysterious," he assured me. "I knew you were planning something, but not that it was this."

"It's reassuring to know I've managed to keep some things a secret, but I'm still doing this," I said firmly. "It's the right thing to do. And you said yourself you hate magic. I'm surprised you didn't suggest breaking it."

"I *do* hate magic," he said. "Very much. What does it say to you that I would keep a magical connection in spite of all of that?"

"It says you take your job too seriously. You need a holiday," I said dryly. "Don't make me insist."

"If I *consent* to this, you won't insist on me taking time off?" he asked.

His deliberate choice of words left me breathless. His eyes snapped with a rare display of anger which quickly dissipated into regret.

"I'm sorry, that was—"

"Yes it was," I snapped. "The fact that you would, for a moment, compare this to what Alistair Dagen did to me…" The worst part about it was that he was right. If I wasn't doing this with his consent, then I was as good as forcing it on him. I never said I wasn't an asshole, but to compare myself to someone so irredeemably disgusting was a whole new low.

"I'm sorry," I said finally. "I had no right to spring this on you. I should have warned you."

He drew himself up, his bodyguard mask firmly in place. "You're the boss. You get to do whatever you want. My job is to make sure no one gets in your way. Including me. I apologise for arguing. It was unprofessional."

I knew that wall he put up around himself all too well. I had no right to feel hurt about it, but I did. Dagen was like the opposite of King Midas. Everything he touched turned to shit. Or maybe it was just me and I was looking for someone else to blame. Either way, a perfectly good working relationship was now tense and I wasn't sure if we would ever be able to go back to the way things were.

"Ben." I wasn't sure what I was going to say. Really, what could I say that would make this any better? "Let's get this over with." I wasn't going to change my mind but the longer we put it off, the harder it would be. There was no point in prolonging this any longer than necessary.

"Yes, boss." His response was almost robotic. Did I sound like that when I was trying to shut everyone out? Probably.

I couldn't look him in the eyes anymore, so I kept my gaze on the floor as we walked back to the office.

We needed to get rid of this bond because, if nothing else, I didn't need him knowing how close I was to crying.

Ivory didn't cry. Ivory was unbreakable. Unshakeable. Nothing got to me. No one got to me. I played those words over and over in my head like a mantra.

"We're ready," I said as we stepped back into the office.

Judging by the expression on Cooper's face, he'd thought we'd gone next door for a quickie. When he saw us back so soon and both with similar expressions, he looked worried.

"Are you guys okay?" he asked. "Did you have a fight?"

"We're fine," I said, my voice tight.

"Nothing to worry about," Ben agreed. To our guests he said, "If you don't mind, my boss would like to get this bond broken." He looked like he wanted to elaborate, but he didn't. Any of the other guys probably would have added something sarcastic, but that wasn't how he rolled.

Harmony rose from her chair and moved to put a hand on my arm. "Are you sure about this?" she asked softly.

"Yes," Paxton agreed. "Be certain, because once this is broken it can only be restored the way it was made in the first place. Bonding stones are hard to find and cost— You could afford it. But they're still hard to find."

"We're sure." I forced myself to look at Ben.

His jaw was set firmly. He could have been the male version of me right now. Maybe stone instead of ice.

"It's been decided," he said.

I felt a flutter of nerves through the bond. For him, it wasn't just about breaking it, it was the proximity to the three witches. He wanted to be anywhere right now but here.

"This shouldn't take long." Paxton took Harmony's hand, and she reached for Jordan's. The air tingled even before Paxton put a hand on my arm. "Take Ben's hand."

I did as he said and noted the look of relief in Ben's eyes that he wouldn't have to touch any of the witches directly. I felt like on some level, I should try to help him get over his prejudice. On the other hand, I didn't trust any black wolf as far as I could spit them. I had no desire or need to get past that prejudice.

I squeezed Ben's hand to reassure him. He squeezed mine back. I knew he would have preferred to snatch his hand back and leave the bond in place. He didn't. He stood perfectly still while Paxton frowned and muttered to himself.

"This is a kind of reverse healing," Paxton said. "Instead of putting things back where they go, I'm taking something away that shouldn't be there. Or at least, something that was added to both of you."

"Is this going to cause any damage?" Ben asked.

That was a good question. One I should have asked before now. Just because Paxton was a doctor didn't mean I could trust him.

"It shouldn't," Paxton said. "If I think it will, I'll

stop and you'll be stuck with the bond forever. You'll have to deal with it."

For a doctor, his bedside manner was shit. On the other hand, it was better than sugar coating things, or flat out lying.

I glanced sideways at Ben. It didn't take a genius, or a bond, to know he would be okay with Paxton failing. Honestly, it wouldn't be the end of the world if we were stuck with it. I mean, they were worse things than a bodyguard who knew exactly where you were at all times.

Now I thought about it—

The bond evaporated and I could no longer feel Ben's emotions. For some reason, I expected it to be a gradual reduction, not the hard slice it was. He was there in one heartbeat and not in the next.

It left me feeling strangely empty.

You know what they say. Be careful what you wish for, you might just get it.

Ben sharply sucked in a breath. Obviously he felt the same immediate response I did.

Paxton lowered his hand and moved away. "There. Done. No damage. You're free to get on with your lives."

Right. No damage. Then why did I feel so empty inside? I couldn't bring myself to entertain the idea that breaking the bond was a mistake. Firstly because I didn't like to second-guess myself, but mostly because it was the right thing for Ben, as far as I was concerned. He might not believe me, or agree, but I did this for him. Because he deserved better than to be stuck with me and my moods.

"Thank you." I let Ben's hand slip out of mine. Something about it felt horribly final.

That was fucking stupid, I told myself. No one should have an empathic link to their employee. Nothing good could ever come of it.

"Ivory," Harmony said tentatively. "Can I have a word with you please? Alone." She gestured towards the other side of the room, which was about as alone as I was prepared to do.

I thought about saying no, but I nodded and stepped over away from all the guys. "What did you need to talk about?"

"I just wanted to be sure you're all right," she said. "You went through a lot and—"

"I'm absolutely fine," I lied. "Now this is done, I can get on with everything. It's nice of you to be concerned about me, but I'm okay."

She gave me a look that clearly said she didn't believe a word of it. She was just as clearly unde-cided as to whether she should push me or not. On one hand, I could decide she didn't need to walk out of here alive. On the other hand, most women who went through what I did, needed a friend. Most men too. I knew Ben and Cooper talked about all sorts of things. So did Ben and Jake. Knowing Cooper, he was also an ear for Hutton.

And me, I had no one. Yeah, okay, a lot of that was by choice. Don't cry me a fucking river. But from time to time, it would be nice to have another woman to talk to.

"If you change your mind and want to have a chat, you know where to find me," she said softly. "If not me, then please talk to someone."

"Maybe I'll get a pet cat," I said dryly.

She smiled. "I hear pets are very good listeners. Better than guys sometimes." She rolled her eyes.

I smiled but couldn't bring myself to laugh. Guys certainly did have their moments.

Her smile faded and she sighed. "I know you're a bit older and probably a lot wiser than me, but I still worry about you. Keeping everything bottled up inside isn't good for you. Being distant from the people around you isn't good either. I know that from experience. Letting people in is scary, but it's worth it."

*Oh yeah,* I thought sarcastically. Who wouldn't

want to end up with someone like Paxton Evans, who kept her locked up in a room for five months? She might need a friend even more than I did. Or a cat. That might be what all of this was about, she needed a friend and was projecting that on to me. That was actually really sad. If that was the case, I felt sorry for her.

There was a good reason I didn't have any friends. I couldn't go for more than a few minutes without questioning their motives. I would always assume they wanted something from me or were trying to advance themselves in some way. I was well aware of my trust issues, but at the end of the day, they kept me alive.

"Just think about what I said, okay?" She patted my arm and moved away.

"We should get going," Jordan said. "It's a long drive back."

"Not until we've experienced the pleasures of the third floor," Paxton said. He gave Harmony a look that would have melted the panties on anyone but me.

Harmony smiled and hooked her arm through Jordan's. "Yes, we can stay a bit longer. You know you want to."

Jordan said not one word of objection as the three of them followed Ben out the door.

"That was really brave of you," Cooper said.

I frowned at him. "What was?"

"Breaking the bond," he said. "It must have been really intense to be connected to someone like that. I love Ben like he's a big brother, but I don't want him in my brain. You know?"

After a moment he added, "I'm not even sure I'd want you in there. No offence. I like not knowing what you're going to say or do next. It keeps things interesting." He looked at me like you would look at a wild animal, not sure if it was going to roll over and show its belly, or claw you to shreds.

At the same time, I could tell he wanted to touch me. He was smart and sensitive enough to understand why I went from so hot to so cold. Unlike Jake, I knew he would stick around whether he was sleeping with me or not. My lifestyle was exciting to him. I was the icing on the cake, but the cake was still pretty tasty.

"I'm glad someone understands," I said. "It was intense."

It was also comforting, and now it was gone, I felt lonelier than ever.

17

"Is it safe?" Hutton stuck his head in the doorway an hour or two later.

"Safe from what?" I looked up from my screen. "Or who?"

He stepped inside and strode over, his hands in his pockets. He shrugged. "Everyone. Specifically Jake. He is never going to not hate my guts, is he?"

I sat back and tucked my legs up underneath me. "I don't think he hates you quite as violently as that. It's just— The past was hard for all of us." The present wasn't all that rosy either, to be honest. With any luck, the future would be better.

"Yeah, no shit." He grabbed a chair, pulled it up to the desk and sat on it backwards. He rested his arms across the back. "It wasn't all Vegemite sandwiches and too many spoonfuls of Nutella for me either."

"Just as well," I said dryly. "Nutella is toxic to dogs." That was a shame, because the chocolate and hazelnut-flavoured spread smelled delicious.

"You know what I mean," he said. "Suburban families and all that shit. Mum and Dad, or Mum and Mum. Or Dad and Dad. Or just one or the other. A pet fish. Friends coming over after school. Riding bikes around the neighbourhood."

I sighed. That was my life for the first eight years. More or less. "Dad and his many girlfriends. Parents fighting. Pressing the button on the answering machine and hearing death threats. Suburban living isn't all rainbows and sunshine."

"All of those things still sound better than being raised to be the enemy to your own people." He rested his chin on his arms. He hadn't shaved in a few days. It was a good look for him.

"Or being raised to roll over onto your back and spread your legs for someone with the last name Dagen." I grimaced.

"I can't imagine you taking that lying down. So to speak." He looked intently at me. "You're made of tougher stuff than that. I doubt they would have gotten out of it without losing a shit load of skin and blood."

"No, they wouldn't have," I agreed. Between Alistair Dagen and his father, life would have been hells.

I cocked my head at him. "You had other kids around you, didn't you?" Hadn't he said he was fostered with a couple of other white wolves?

"Yeah, but everything was a competition. Every chance they got, they pitted us against each other. If we were too slow, we were punished. If we weren't careful enough, we were punished. Eventually, we started to see each other as the enemy. It wasn't that I was too slow, it was that they were faster than me. Maybe they pushed themselves a little harder so I would get punished. Looking back, that seems really stupid. But at the time, that was how it was."

"That sounds lonely," I said softly. That might explain my attraction to him. We both went through things the others would never truly understand. The absolute desperation to survive, but the almost equally absolute certainty the black wolves would destroy us. There were days I almost accepted the future they planned for me. Right up until the moment the hammer fell on my virgin auction. Until I saw the look of fury on Alistair's father's face. He and his son were really good at one thing: assuming they had more time than they actually did. Had they realised it, things would have been worse for me.

Hutton shrugged. "I can deal with loneliness. It was the part about doing shitty things to other white wolves that I struggle with. Sometimes I wished Gus Dagen would beat me to death. So I didn't have to keep doing things." His eyes glazed over as he thought back over the memories.

"Other times, I wished I dared to beat him to death. If the other guys and I got our shit together, he wouldn't have been able to stop us. We were just too fucking scared. Half the time we would jump at our own shadows."

I put a hand on his arm. "I'm sorry that happened to you. I wish I'd been old enough to stop everything sooner."

He snorted lightly. "You changed everything for a generation of white wolves, and you're still not satisfied that you did enough? Believe me, you did plenty. The gods know there were other people who could have done something."

"Like Jake?" I guessed. "He didn't like sitting on his hands, waiting. He hated himself for it. He still does."

"That makes two of us." Hutton grinned.

I socked him lightly on the arm. "Sooner or later,

one of you is going to have to let up on the other one. If only so you can work together in peace. I guess I could always fire one of you." I shrugged.

"As long as it's him," Hutton said. "You would come to regret firing me. I'm awesome." He wiggled his brows.

I shook my head at him. "Of course you are."

Guys.

"Seriously though, none of us came through all of that unscathed. Ben's parents fled the state before they died. Left everything they had behind. They had to start over, in Tasmania. That's the same story for a lot of the staff here. That or they grew up in remote parts of New South Wales, or on the border with other states. Some of them even grew up in Queensland or the Northern Territory, because they knew they'd be safer there than here."

"Desperate times call for desperate measures," he said.

"That they do," I agreed.

"Is that why you're trying to push all of us away?" he asked. "Desperate times?"

"You noticed too, hmmm?" I rearranged my legs so I was sitting cross-legged on the chair. "You of all people should understand why."

"Because the Onyx Ridge pack are experts at

pitting us against each other," he said. "You don't want them to do anything to us in order to get to you. Or vice versa. But there's one thing I've learnt in my long, long life, and it's that being lonely sucks. Yeah, there are worse things, but there are better things. You have this whole big bad wolf vibe going on, but I know for a fact that you would prefer to save the huffing and puffing for the bedroom. Or the couch. Or the desk. Or—"

"Okay, okay, I get the idea." I rolled my eyes at him. He wasn't wrong. I much preferred my huffing and puffing to involve cocks and orgasms.

I frowned. "You think everything Asshole has done, and keeps doing, is because he wants me to push you guys away? To isolate me from everyone else?"

"Is his last name Dagen?" Hutton asked rhetorically. "They get off on two things." He held up a finger. "One, power. And two, mind fucks. If they can combine those two into one, then they're as happy as a pig in shit. Let's be real here for a moment. He would have really gotten off on seeing you devastated over me and Ben dying. Ben in particular, because of that bond. That would have given him the mother of all hard ons. If your friends hadn't arrived just in time…"

I nodded. "Yes, I know what would have happened." It would have been brutal. "But caring about anyone sets the stage for that to happen again."

"So does being alone," he argued. "You're stronger with our support than without it. Let me ask you this." He paused for a moment to gather his thoughts. "Could you have done all of this," he gestured around the room, "without Jake's help?"

"Now you want to give him credit," I teased gently. "No. I couldn't have done this without him. Without his money or his support."

"Are you worried that if you push him away hard enough, he could withdraw his support? What if he decided to go against you somehow?" He raised an eyebrow at me in speculation.

"He would never do that," I said with certainty. Of course, now the seed of doubt was in my mind. Jake and I at war with each other would make this thing between Dagen and I look like a water fight. It would be ugly and bloody, and destroy us both.

"Probably not," Hutton agreed. "The point is, when you're all in with someone, you're all in. And as for us four guys, we're all in with you. Whether you want us to be or not. But I hope you want us to be."

He stood and stepped away from the chair. "Just think about what I said. Okay?"

"I make no guarantees," I said. "But I'll try."

"That's all I ask." He slipped back out the door.

I stood and walked over to the window to stretch my legs. At least a million conflicting thoughts bounced around in my brain. That was nothing unusual, but he'd added a couple of extra ones.

Men.

I saw movement in the corner of my eye and Hutton's reflection appeared in the window a moment later. I turned around.

"Did you come back to give me some more pearls of wisdom?" I asked.

"No." He shook his head, then put his arms around me and lowered his mouth to mine. The kiss he gave me was soft, but firm. He tasted of cola and cinnamon. An interesting combination.

He deepened the kiss and slid his hands up my back and twined his fingers in my hair.

Without thinking, I kissed him back. It wasn't the sweet, naïve kisses Cooper gave. Or the possessive alpha kisses of Jake. Or the gentle, steady kisses of Ben.

This was the kiss of a man who didn't want to hurt me or be hurt, but who desperately needed to connect with another person. Someone who had spent most of his life alone and lonely. Someone who, in spite of his probably better judgement, decided to invest his heart in me.

And somewhere deep in that kiss, I forgot to think and just let myself feel.

I have no idea how we got to the couch or which one of us led the other there, but the next thing I knew, he was lowering me onto it.

I lay back without our lips breaking contact for even a second.

He settled in on top of me and knelt between my knees. He slipped his hands under my shirt and pushed it up off my belly. Still without breaking off the kiss, he pulled me up to a sitting position.

Now he only broke off long enough to pull my shirt over my head and toss it aside. He pushed me back down gently and reclaimed my mouth.

I don't know how, but he managed to unhook my bra and slide it off my arms without even lifting my back off the couch again. Later, I would have to figure out how he did that.

His hands wandered lightly up and down my stomach and over my breasts. He traced circles around my nipples without touching them.

Even that light touch was enough to drive me wild. My body was already aching for more.

Finally, he broke off the kiss and worked his way down from my neck, to my chest, to my breasts. There, he traced circles around my nipples with his tongue. Only after a few minutes did he finally take my nipple into his mouth and start to suck.

"Mmm," he murmured against my sensitive skin. "You're so soft."

I hadn't heard that one before, but it was a compliment I could own. When your breasts are a decent size, you might as well. Right?

He lavished so much attention on my nipples, I started to think the bond transferred to him somehow. I put it down to a lifetime of having to be vigilant. With that, comes being observant. I saw it in Ben and now in Hutton. Jake too. Cooper just rolled with whatever felt good. It sucked that anything good came from the past, but that didn't mean I wouldn't enjoy it.

He kissed and licked his way down my stomach, taking a moment to lightly kiss my abdomen. There was no scar there now, Paxton had gotten rid of it, but Hutton had the general area right. And the sentiment.

He hooked his thumbs into the waistband of my

track pants and worked them down off my hips and down my legs. I kicked them off my feet. My panties followed.

He slid off the couch and knelt beside it, his hands on my thighs. His brown eyes on mine, he lowered his mouth to my pussy and started to give it the same attention he'd given my nipples. He licked my folds and sucked my clit until my breath was coming in tiny pants.

His hands slid up and down my thighs and around to grip my ass. He picked it up off the couch and dove in a little deeper.

I pressed my hands to either side of me. Each breath was accompanied by a moan and a rise in my desire.

"I'm going to come," I said.

I expected him to tell me to wait, but his eyes smiled at me and he went on licking vigourously.

I arched my back as the first wave of delicious orgasm washed over me. Followed closely by a second. Then a third. The entire world stopped for a full two to three minutes. The only thing that was left was his skilled tongue and a million fireworks.

Finally, he let me go and I slumped back down on the couch.

"Holy fucking gods," I breathed. "That was amazing."

He crawled back up the couch and once again knelt between my knees. He kissed my mouth and I tasted myself on his lips.

"I wanted to hear you sing and you didn't disappoint," he whispered.

"Is that all you want?" I reached down between us to unfasten his pants and push them down.

"Since you're asking…" He kicked off his pants and revealed a very big, very hard cock.

"What—"

He shrugged. "I hated myself. I tried to think of the most painful thing I could do to myself, that might bring enjoyment to someone else some day."

In a line down his cock were four, no, five, piercings, parallel to each other like a silver ladder.

"Did that hurt?" I asked. I reached out to lightly touch one.

"Not as much as I hoped," he admitted. "It actually feels pretty good. More sensitive and intense."

"It's hot," I told him. My body throbbed just thinking how he'd feel sliding in and out of me.

"You're hot," he replied. He eyed my mouth speculatively.

My response was involuntary, but immediate. I shuddered and a hint of panic started to rise.

"Oh shit," he said softly. "I'm sorry. I didn't mean to—" He started to roll off me.

I put a hand on his arm to stop him. "You didn't do anything. I want you. Only…" I swallowed. "In my pussy, not in my mouth. Okay?"

He nodded his understanding, but his brown eyes showed a flash of anger. He would tear Dagen in two with his bare hands if he was here right now.

"Okay," he said gently. "Whatever you need. If you want me to stop, just say the word and I will."

I flashed a brief smile, then pulled him back down on top of me and hooked my legs around him. "If you do anything I don't like, you will hear about it." That went for in and out of the bedroom.

He chuckled. "I have no doubt about that, babe." He wriggled his hips a little to get himself into position, then carefully, with his eyes on mine to engage my reaction, he pressed his thick, laddered length into me.

The moment my eyes widened, he stopped to let me adjust to him. He was definitely the biggest guy I ever fucked, even without the piercings. My muscles took a few moments to stretch and relax.

When I finally did, he slid in a little further.

"Gods, you feel so tight," he said breathlessly.

"You feel so big," I replied. I had never felt quite this full before. It was pretty wonderful.

"I don't want to brag." He grinned. "Are you okay?"

There was that question again. I didn't mind it so much in this context. I was lying naked on a couch with a hot guy on top of me, his cock deep inside my body. I was more than okay.

"I'm wonderful," I said.

"Yes you are." He kissed my mouth, then slowly started to thrust, his eyes half closed in obvious appreciation. "Absolutely perfect." Gradually his strokes became faster, but never rushed. Either he was the kind of guy who likes to take his time, or he wanted to be sure not to hurt me.

Maybe both.

His piercings felt like ridges, which massaged my slick core with every movement. I never felt anything like it before. It was pretty fucking amazing.

I rocked my hips in time with his and clenched my muscles around him.

His breathing became ragged.

Careful not to dislodge him, I rolled us both over so I was straddling his hips.

He put his hands on my waist and didn't even break his rhythm.

I pressed my palms to his muscular chest, half closed my eyes and rode him with his cock so deep it almost hurt. His ladder rubbed my g spot inside, and at the same time, my clit rubbed against him on the outside. It was like the world evaporated, leaving behind one one sense; that of touch.

Feeling.

Heightened, intense, deep desire.

"Mmm, yeah." His breathing was deeper and faster. Every so often it would hitch. He was close to coming himself.

I watched his face. I wanted to see him and feel him come. I loved knowing I could do that to a guy.

Especially like this. I was in complete control. He surrendered everything willingly, with no reservation.

I slowed down a little to draw out his pleasure.

One of his eyebrows rose in response, but he didn't say anything. I wasn't sure he was capable of words right now. Neither was I.

I tried to stop myself, but I came again.

If the first three were fireworks, then the fourth was New Year's Eve, with a dose of Australia Day thrown in for good measure. I was absolutely lost in the rush of heat and blood and pleasure.

Through the pounding in my ears, I heard his groans and grunts and felt him grind up into me as he came.

When he managed a word, it was just a long, low, "Baaaaabe."

Maybe I didn't mind him calling me that after all.

Finally, I sagged down onto him, panting and sweaty.

"Wow," he said breathlessly. "You're even more amazing than I imagined. And what I imagined was pretty fucking incredible."

"Thank goodness for that," I said softly. "I would hate for you to hype me up to yourself only to find out I'm a bad fuck." Yeah, that would suck. I had some pride left.

He chuckled. "That is something you could never be. You're far too wonderful."

"You're going to make me blush," I said to his chest. I could lie there all day. Maybe sleep there all night. Unfortunately, I couldn't. We had plans tonight. An event I couldn't miss, as much as I wanted to.

"We should probably get up and have a shower," I said reluctantly.

"Together?" he asked.

Okay, maybe I could get up after all.

At some point though, I was going to have to figure a few things out. A lot of things.

For one thing, Hutton was right about Dagen wanting me to push the guys away and isolate myself.

On the other hand, I made that choice for a reason. The fact I was lying here right now with Hutton strongly suggested I wasn't very good at sticking to the choices I made. Or maybe subconsciously I knew they were shitty choices.

Yeah, I really had some thinking to do.

18

ALL FIVE OF us were absolutely smoking hot that night. The guys wore dark suits and crisp white shirts. Cooper wore a brightly coloured tie, while the other three had more subdued colours. They even had shiny shoes on.

I wore a long, white gown that shimmered when I moved. It was higher in the front than what I usually wore, but dipped down low at the back. Of course, it had a long split down the side, and the fabric clung to my curves like an opaque condom. Without all the rubber and need for lube.

I straightened my hair and left it out to fall down my back. As always, a pair of designer heels finished the outfit.

"Stay close to Ivory," Jake said. "This might be a

charity concert, but there will be a few dubious people here."

"Like us?" Hutton asked.

Jake gave him a dark look, but nodded. "Yes, like us. Just not as hot."

"We look pretty good, don't we?" Cooper grinned.

I glanced at Ben, who hadn't said a word all night. It was normal for him to stay quiet while he was on the job, unless he needed to say something, but I missed the sound of his deep voice.

He gave the slightest nod of agreement, then went back to watching the crowds.

It was warm out tonight. The Harbour looked beautiful. The Opera House, the location for the night's concert, was lit up and shining. A quartet on stage played something by Vivaldi. A shit load of rich people had turned up to raise money for orphaned children. It was a practically perfect evening.

For a while.

That was before I saw Alistair Dagen. He was surrounded, as usual, by a contingent of goons.

Not just any goons, I quickly realised. The three who held me down, and another two who held my arms while their companions chased Ben and Hutton. There was no chance their inclusion at this event this evening was coincidental. It was just another mind fuck.

"You look beautiful tonight, Elodie," Asshole said smoothly. "Although, I'm surprised you came. I thought you would have some rubble to sift through."

"Fuck off, Alistair," I replied. I wasn't even going to bother with niceties. If it wasn't for the fact we were surrounded by a few hundred people, I would shift and rip his head off. The five of us could take on the six of them.

He started to clap slowly. "Well done. Such an intelligent, eloquent response."

I rolled my eyes at him. "I can't be bothered wasting brain cells on a worthless slug like you."

"That's better." He nodded. "Although, your insults could use a bit of work. Maybe I could give you some pointers, bitch."

I bared my teeth at him.

Before I could even speak, he said, "I know, don't call you bitch. But it fits so perfectly. Especially if I add the words 'in heat,' to it. Still fucking your body-guard? Or just your lapdog? Oh wait, then there's your little virgin boytoy. And Hutton, I'm so glad to see you still alive. That means I get the fun of killing you again."

"Fuck off, Dagen," Hutton said.

"Yeah, what he said." Cooper jerked a thumb toward Hutton. "If anyone is killing anyone else around here, it's me killing you."

Dagen chuckled. "Elodie, you should probably put a leash on that puppy. Or better yet, a *collar*."

Jake yawned loudly. "Are you done? None of us are impressed with your bullshit." To Cooper he said, "You'll have to get in line to kill this asshole. I'm at the front of it."

He turned back to Dagen. "Were you the bully at school too? What kind of man kidnaps women? Oh, right, the kind with a really, really, *really* small cock."

Dagen gave him a nasty smile. "It's not that small. Just ask your bitch there." He turned that expression on me. "That reminds me, when I was going through a bunch of security footage, I found a little something. I thought you'd like a copy." He held up his phone and tapped the screen.

A moment later mine pinged. Every single part of me said to ignore it. Everything except my stupid curiosity. The part of me that assumed he had footage of Ben and I fucking and thought that would embarrass me in some way. Or upset Jake or the other guys.

I pulled my phone out of my purse and clicked on the screen.

The moment I did it I regretted it. The vision was a little grainy but the camera had captured the moment the three goons pushed me to my knees. My eyes were wide with horror. Dagen stepped over to me. Undid his pants. From this angle, no one could tell it was him, but everything else was clear enough.

I closed the screen before I could see any more. My hand was trembling. The air became thicker. No, that was just panic rising, making it harder to breathe. My head felt light.

"You're welcome," Asshole said smoothly. "Then I figured—why not share?" He pressed his screen again.

Jake's phone pinged

Then Cooper's.

Hutton's.

Ben's.

Then all around me, phones were pinging. The sound was like something out of a horror movie.

The guys didn't move, but all around me people looked at their screens, then at me. Some looked disgusted, but one or two looked amused like they thought I got what I deserved.

"Excuse me," I muttered. I turned to shove my way through the crowds, my head down as if that would stop people from recognising me.

I heard the guys calling out after me, but I also heard Alistair Dagen's laughter. That rang in my ears louder than anything.

I hurried towards the car and fished my keys out of my purse.

Barely able to breathe, I unlocked it and slipped inside. I pulled off my heels and threw them over into the passenger side footwell.

"Going somewhere?" Hutton slipped into the passenger seat.

"Away from here." My hand was trembling so hard I could hardly get the key into the ignition. Jake might have a point about cars that start with the press of a button.

"Should you leave your bodyguards behind?" He clicked his seatbelt into place.

"You're here," I pointed out. I managed to get the key in and started the car. I backed out of the parking space faster than I probably should have.

I saw the flash of Hutton's phone screen.

"Just letting them know I'm with you and you're okay," he said. "Whatever he sent, I deleted it without looking. The other guys would have too.

And everyone else, who gives a shit what they think?"

"I don't." I wound through the busy carpark and out onto the main road. "I just don't like being humiliated like that. It was bad enough it happened without everyone knowing about it."

No one who actually watched could see his face. I couldn't even point the finger at him. Even the faces of his men weren't clear. Just mine.

Rain started to sprinkle, covering the windscreen in glittering drops. I turned on the windscreen wipers.

With any luck, it would pour and Asshole would get drenched.

I wished he *had* shared footage of Ben and I together. That would have been humiliating for us both, but at least it wasn't evidence I wasn't invincible. Everyone would look at me differently now. They knew I had weaknesses. They would try to exploit them.

Or they would look at me with pity in their eyes.

Panic started to rise again, but this time I let it. I couldn't have held it back if I tried. It swamped me like a flood of cold, trembling fear.

I couldn't let him break me. I wouldn't. But he got to me with this stunt.

I wasn't sure who I hated more right now, him or myself.

"Maybe you should slow down a bit," Hutton said.

"Maybe you shouldn't have gotten into the car with me." Fuck, even my voice was shaking. I felt like a trembling mess coming apart at the seams.

I would make Alistair Dagen pay for this if it was the last thing I ever did. I would make him hurt, make him suffer and then I would kill him. Jake wasn't first in line for that honour. I was.

"What the fuck?" Hutton shouted a fraction of a second before I saw a huge shape step out on the road.

Two enormous eyes turned towards us and blinked.

"Shit." I rammed my foot down onto the break, but we were going too fast and the road was too wet.

The car went into a skid. It hit the side of the road, flipped and started to roll over and over and over.

It finally came to a stop on its roof as the rain started to pour down in torrents.

THANK YOU FOR READING! Grab the final instalment of Ivory's story- Elodie

# ABOUT THE AUTHOR

Maggie Alabaster writes reverse harem and, paranormal, sci-fi and fantasy romance.

She lives in NSW, Australia with one spouse, two daughters, one dog, and countless birds.

Sign up for my newsletter! Sign Up!

Join my reader group! Join here!

Follow me on Bookbub! Click here to follow me!

Check out my website- www.maggiealabaster.com

ALSO BY MAGGIE ALABASTER

Ruck Boys

Filthy Ruck

Hard Ruck

Twisted Ruck

Bad Ruck

Dirty Ruck

Deadly Ruck


Sparrow and the Mafia Kings

Possessive

Ruined

Corrupted


Pucking Dark Hearts

Pucking Hearts Collide

Pucking Forbidden Hearts

Pucking Hardened Hearts


Dusk Bay Demons

Puck Drop

Breakaway

Power Play


Brutal Academy

Book 1 Heartless

Book 2 Cruel

Book 3 Vengeful


Court of Blood and Binding

Book 1 Song of Scent and Magic

Book 2 Crown of Mist and Heat

Book 3 Sword of Balm and Shadow

Book 4 Whisper of Frost and Flame


Dark Masque

Book 1 Bait

Book 2 Prey

Book 3 Trap


Saving Abbie

Book 1 Pitch

Book 2 Pound

Book 3 Session

Book 4 Muse

Book 5 Rhythm

Book 6 Encore

Novella Venomous

Saving Abbie books 1-4

Saving Abbie books 4-6 + Venomous


Ruthless Claws

Book 1 Ivory

Book 2 Crimson

Book 3 Elodie


Harmony's Magic

Book 1 Summoned by Fire

Book 2 Summoned by Fate

Book 3 Summoned by Desire


Shifter's Vault

Book 1 Discarded

Book 2 Deceived

Book 3 Disgraced


My Alien Mates

Book 1 Star Warriors

Book 2 Star Defenders

Book 3 Star Protectors

Academy of Modern Magic

Book 1 Digital Magic

Book 2 Virtual Magic

Book 3 Logical Magic

Complete Collection


Summer's Harem

Book 1: Shimmer

Book 2: Glimmer

Book 3: Flicker

Complete collection


Short reads

Taken by the Snowmen

Jingle All the Way

Also by Maggie Alabaster and Erin Yoshikawa

Caught by the Tide

Book 1–Pursued by Shadows

Book 2 Pursued by Darkness

Book 3 Pursued by Monsters

www.ingramcontent.com/pod-product-compliance
Lightning Source LLC
Chambersburg PA
CBHW062010190726
48283CB00002BA/632